THE TOY

THE TOY

CLAIRE THOMPSON

BLUE MOON BOOKS
NEW YORK

THE TOY

Published by
Blue Moon Books
An Imprint of Avalon Publishing Group, Incorporated
245 West 17th Street, 11th floor
New York, NY 10011-5300

First Blue Moon Books Edition 2006

ISBN-10: 1-56201-518-4
ISBN-13: 978-1-56201-518-3

9 8 7 6 5 4 3 2

Printed in the USA
Distributed by Publishers Group West

THE TOY

Chapter 1

THE ABDUCTION

Gina was a nice girl. A little plump—pleasingly plump, her fiancé Dwayne assured her—a little prissy, very proper. Never having gone to college, at twenty-two Gina lived at home with her parents while awaiting her marriage to Dwayne, whom she had known since kindergarten. They attended the same church and it had never occurred to her to want someone different. Not that she actually wanted Dwayne, whatever that meant, but her parents assured her it was God's will that she marry and have children and take her place in the world at Dwayne's side. That was good enough for her.

Gina didn't seek adventure, but she did have a wild side. That is what her parents believed, at any rate, and they were probably right, though Gina hadn't yet figured this out about herself. But she did volunteer work on the "wrong side of the tracks" as her father said, helping those less fortunate than herself, working in a Christian Outreach Center two days a week from 9:00 to 5:00. This was wild behavior in her father's book, but he tolerated it because it was for a higher cause.

This fall Tuesday she had been delayed at work, as several staff members had been out sick. She didn't get out until 8:00 and it was already dark. Gina pulled her practical woolen coat tighter around herself as the wind whipped the air at her bus stop. She was alone and not certain when the bus would come, this being so much later than she was used to being out. Soon she would be home and mom would make her a nice cup of cocoa and she would read her novel, say her prayers, and go to sleep. Her life was, if a little dull, very predictable, and Gina liked order. All that was about to change.

"Excuse me, ma'am."

Gina looked up and saw a disheveled looking woman, too skinny, with something not quite right about the eyes. Drugs, Gina thought, mentally shaking her head in disapproval. But she was a polite girl, and she smiled and nodded toward the young woman.

"My baby." The woman pointed toward a little car parked on the other side of the road. She didn't elaborate.

"Pardon?"

"My baby. She's stuck in the car seat. I can't open it. She's crying like crazy. Would you try?"

What an odd request! The woman didn't look overly distraught, as Gina would have been if her own child were stuck somewhere. Must be the drugs! And that poor baby stuck! Gina's naturally generous nature gave way to any misgivings and she hurried over with the woman to help the baby.

They got to the car and the woman opened the back door. Gina leaned in, expecting to hear a squalling infant. Before her eyes had adjusted to the dark interior of the car, she suddenly felt herself pushed into the back seat. She fell forward with a startled squeal as the door slammed shut behind her. The front window rolled down, a hand extending with an envelope, which the supposed mother took before fading into the autumn gloom.

Gina screamed, and a hand clamped itself over her mouth, muffling the sound. The car engine started and the little car drove away with Gina a prisoner inside. She was terrified. As she thrashed and jerked, trying to get herself free, the hands on her tightened, and then someone hit her hard on the back of the head with something heavy. Gina fell back, limp and silent, into his arms.

• • •

When Gina came to, she was in a room. It was totally dark, except for a crack of light showing under what must have been the door. Her first conscious thought was of pain—a dull throb at the back of her head where she had been hit. As she came fully awake she realized she was sitting upright in a chair. Her heart began to beat wildly against her ribs as consciousness rushed back and she realized she had been kidnapped. Kidnapped! Who could possibly want to kidnap her, and why? Trying to lift her hand to brush hair from her face, Gina realized her hands were tied behind the chair. Her legs were tied to the legs of the chair, forcing her to sit in a most unladylike position, the rope holding her at the knee and ankle. Her head was pounding and it took her a moment to take in the most horrible fact of all! She was naked!

Except for a crisscross of thick rope that covered her body, Gina's pink, plump flesh was exposed to all the world, or at least whomever had kidnapped her. She felt heat suffusing her features, creeping down her chest; she was horrified at the thought of someone seeing her like this. She was never naked, ever, except in the shower. She never looked at herself and certainly didn't allow Dwayne to do so! Not until marriage, she reminded him on those rare occasions when his passion got the best of him and a chaste kiss threatened to go too far.

But now she was naked, her small, high breasts exposed, the rosy pink nipples jutting between the ropes that cruelly cut into her skin. Her sex was exposed, and try as she might, she couldn't budge to shut her legs. The sheer embarrassment of being naked was so acute it completely took over any fear of being kidnapped or killed.

She began to cry, little hysterical mews and gulps, as tears welled out of her eyes, overflowing on soft round cheeks. Her cries changed to a startled scream when someone behind her said, "Ah, finally coming out of it, eh? Gordon smacked you a little too hard. I warn him that he doesn't know his own strength. But you should be okay in a day or two. No permanent damage." As he spoke, the man flicked on the overhead lights.

Gina squinted in the bright fluorescent light, trying to focus. As her vision cleared, she realized she was in a room that was completely empty, and covered in mirrors from floor to ceiling. "Please!" Gina cried. "Please! What are you going to do to me? Why am I here? Please, oh please let me go!" Her voice broke as she sobbed in fear.

"Relax, sugar. We aren't going to kill you. We don't plan to, that is, as long as you do what you're told. Just relax. You are going to be staying with us for a long time. You can make it real hard on yourself, or you can relax and enjoy it. I think we're going to have us a whole lot of fun, Gina. Just you, me, and Gordon. You're our new pet. We got tired of the old one."

Gina was unable to take in what he was saying. As the man walked around in front of her, Gina squeezed her eyes shut, praying with all her might. But the prayers must have fallen on deaf ears because when she opened her eyes, the man was still standing right in front of her. He was tall and lean, dressed in a white cotton T-shirt and jeans. His thick dark hair was cut short.

He knelt in front of Gina, his face crinkled in amusement. She screamed, her eyes still squeezed shut, when she felt his hand on her thigh. Slowly the large, rough fingers moved toward her exposed sex. The fingers moved past her pubic curls and down to the bare little pussy below. Her screaming became a high-pitched wail. The man withdrew his hand and slapped her, hard, across the face. Then again, on the other cheek, stunning her into silence.

"Come on now, sweetheart. Sorry I had to do that, but you're becoming a pain in the ass. If you don't shut your mouth, I'm afraid I'm going to have to tape it shut. We mustn't disturb Gordon. Won't do at all. One more sound out of you, except for answers to direct questions, and I will duct tape your mouth. Do you understand?"

Terrified, Gina nodded mutely. Her breathing was ragged, and she gasped when he touched her pussy again. When his finger entered her, the largest thing to ever penetrate her virgin sex, she forgot herself and screamed again.

Feigning disgust, the man slapped her again, so hard her ears were ringing. He left for a moment and came back, the duct tape in hand. Pulling off a large silver rectangle and biting it with his teeth, he pressed the sticky tape tightly over Gina's mouth, muffling her cries.

"You want to do things the hard way, Gina, then that's what we'll do. Gordon'll like that. He likes to *break the fillies*, as he says. He likes the wild ones. They never stay wild, though, Gina. Just remember that. Once Gordon has a go at you, you'll learn to behave, I can promise you that."

Gina's eyes were round as plates as she stared at the man. He knew her name! As if reading her mind he said, "We have your purse, sweetheart. We have your license. We know where you work, where you live, what your boyfriend looks like. We'll know a whole lot more than that eventually. But right now we have all the time in the world. The fun is just beginning, baby." Blessed darkness claimed Gina, as she fainted dead away.

• • •

When Gina again regained consciousness, she was no longer tied to the chair. Instead she found herself lying on the floor, handcuffed, with a long, thick chain secured to a rung on the floor. She was still naked, tethered on a thin mattress. Her mouth was still taped shut. Cautiously she sat up, struggling to balance without the use of her hands. The room was harshly lit and all around her she saw her own naked and manacled form. She fell back down on the thin pillow, moaning through the tape. What was going to happen to her?

As if in answer, Gina heard the click of a lock opening and then the door swung open. It wasn't the same man as before. This must be Gordon. He was smaller than the first man, and much fairer, with sandy blond hair and dark eyes. He looked almost boyish, except for his expression, which was intense. There was no easy smile on his face and his eyes seemed to burn. His mouth was thin-lipped and cruel. Unlike the casual dress of the first man, he was wearing a blazer and dark pants, precisely creased. He didn't say a word to the chained young woman before him.

Kneeling, he leaned his face to hers. Taking a corner of the tape, with a yank he pulled it from her delicate skin. Gina cried out, her manacled hands touching the reddened flesh around her mouth. Gordon slapped away her fingers. Taking her head in his hands, he kissed her, hard, on the mouth. Gina squealed, trying to pull away. "Don't resist me." His voice was flat, calm, precise. It sounded British. He slapped her, very hard, on one cheek. Her chained hands flew up to her hot cheek as she gasped.

"This isn't play time with little boyfriend. Forget about your life. It's over." He ignored the sob. "I don't mean you're going to die, stupid; I mean the life you knew is over. You're my toy now. That is all you are. My pet. My slave, my whore. I will teach you to obey. You may come to love it; you may come to hate it. That's of no concern to me. None at all. But I will tell you this." He leaned close again, so that she could feel his hot breath on her face. "Don't you ever pull away, don't you ever try to resist me again, for any reason, or you will pay. Dearly. Am I understood?"

His voice was cold, and though his lips formed a smile, it didn't make it to his eyes. Gina felt a hot, sharp finger of dread drag through her innards. She felt the swoon of a faint coming over her again. Gordon grabbed her by a fistful of hair and said, "If you faint again, Gina, I'll revive you in a way you'll find most unpleasant. Enough Victorian bullshit. Stand up."

Gina stared at him, her eyes wide, her mouth trembling. But she knew instinctively that there was no room for negotiation. Stumbling a little, the poor naked young woman stood up next to the mattress.

Gordon took her chained wrists firmly in one hand and raised her arms high above her head. Before she could react, he had secured the chain to a conveniently placed hook in the ceiling.

Gina squeezed her eyes shut, moaning in fear. "Nice tits, if you go in for that sort of thing." Playfully, Gordon tweaked one of Gina's nipples. The nipples were small and pale pink against her even paler white skin. From his pocket Gordon produced two wooden clothespins. "A bit small," he said critically, as he twisted one nipple between rough fingers. Gina gasped, but when she pulled back, it only increased the tension on her nipple. She tried to stay still. Gordon released the nipple, which now stood at attention, in contrast to the other nipple. Gordon liked symmetry, and so he pulled and twisted the other nipple until it too stood at dark pink attention.

"Good. They enlarge nicely when provoked," he said aloud, though he wasn't speaking to the girl. She was simply an object for his present amusement. "Now, I've devised a clever little game. It's called rotation. I use it when I don't want to mark someone, or when I really want to watch them suffer, over and over and over again. Every time that pin is rotated the pain increases significantly. The advantage of this particular torture is that it inflicts severe pain without actually cutting the flesh. Much more effective than clamps, and certainly more cost effective." He smiled cruelly, and while Gina watched, eyes wide in terror, he pushed one clothespin open. Pulling her nipple taut and away from her body, he let the clothespin snap down onto the extended nubbin.

Gina screamed and jerked away, but the clothespin was tightly coiled and stayed clamped on her nipple, bobbing slightly as she pulled back. "Very nice," Gordon nodded, pleased with the effect. Then he took the second pin and quickly pulled her other nipple, letting the pin snap closed upon it just as he had the first.

"Stop! Stop, stop, stop! What are you doing to me! Please, God! It hurts! Stop!"

"It's supposed to hurt. Now shut your mouth, or I'll use that nasty duct tape on it again. Do you want that?"

Gina shook her head, quieting to a whimper. Her eyes were moist and pleading. Gordon felt his cock stiffen in his pants. He loved that look of helpless terror. He loved knowing he was the cause of it. And now for the real pain. Taking each clip in hand, he squeezed, releasing the grip on Gina's breasts. As the blood flowed back into her now tender nipples, she hissed involuntarily.

Turning the pins at a new angle, Gordon clamped her flesh again.

After about fifteen seconds, he released the pins, and again Gina's nerves were stimulated and she felt the pain afresh. Over and over again he clamped and released her poor nipples, till they had gone from pale pink to bright cherry red. Gina was moaning, her head back, eyes closed. Her nipples looked so pretty and erect that Gordon couldn't resist a little bite to each one. Now they glistened with his kiss. His cock was painful in his pants and he adjusted it slightly.

Gina looked almost asleep now, slack in her bonds. But her heavy breathing gave her away. He would wake her up with his next remark. "Now I'm going to give you your first whipping. At least I assume it's your first?" His laugh was low and cruel. Producing a small riding crop from his jacket, Gordon lightly smacked Gina's pert little breasts, thoughtfully avoiding the distended nipples. Gina begged him to let her down, but her cry fell on deaf, or at least indifferent, ears.

The sound of the hard leather square of the crop against soft skin made a smacking echo in the mirrored room. Each smack was punctuated by Gina's cry. From all angles the mirrors reflected the naked plump young woman, dark hair tumbling about her shoulders, high breasts raised further by her arms extended over her head. Gordon brought the crop down against her ass, making it jiggle. He liked to see the big ass turning pink as it bounced. Gina twitched and tried to move out of the way, but of course she could not, bound in chains and restrained as she was.

When Gordon began to use the crop on her back, Gina's cries doubled in volume and pain. Her ass, at least, was protected by ample padding, but her back was more sensitive and the stinging blows were peppering her flesh. As she turned in an effort to avoid the crop, it caught her neatly across one nipple. Her cries became a wail of agony and tears began to seep from her eyes, which were squeezed shut in fear. Gordon knew that smack to the nipple must have felt like fire. But he also knew that this was not a particularly severe beating—any moderately trained slave could have taken it in silence without a whimper. Except for that one blow to the aching nipple.

But Gina was not a slave, not yet. She hadn't even begun to imagine what it was to suffer. But she would learn, and quickly. Gordon was a devoted teacher. He laughed at this silent description of himself and began to whip her harder, smacking her belly, her sex, her back, her ass, her thighs. Gina began to dance involuntarily, squealing and jumping in an effort to avoid the sharp, stinging blows. She was crying and begging, but this only seemed to spur Gordon on, and his blows became harder and harder, leaving angry red marks all over the virgin's body.

When at last he stopped, Gina was bathed in sweat. She felt a warm stream of something rushing down her leg and, horrified, realized she had wet herself. Gordon realized it too. "You filthy pig," he snarled, his voice dripping with disgust. Roughly he pushed her to the mattress, leaving her wet with her own urine, to cry herself to sleep.

"Tomorrow," he promised, as he locked the door behind him, "your real training begins."

Chapter 2

THE KISS

Hours had passed. Gina realized she must have fallen asleep, because as she squinted her eyes open, the fog of dreams momentarily confused her and she thought she was at home in her own safe bed. It even smelled like home, and the scent of baking brought images of her mother's warm cheerful kitchen to her mind. But the chains on her wrists and the damp urine-splashed mattress beneath her naked body reminded her with instant and miserable certainty that she was not at home.

Struggling to sit up, Gina saw that a tray had been laid next to her, with a dishtowel covering it. Tentatively Gina reached out and removed the towel. Three warm muffins nestled in a basket and there was an empty mug and a little pitcher of what smelled like hot coffee. There were even a little ceramic creamer and sugar bowl. Gina realized she was starving, and marveled at herself that she could even think about food when she might be murdered at any moment.

Always a practical girl, she decided she might as well die full as hungry. Reaching for a muffin, she took a large bite. It was unbelievably delicious, with fresh blueberries in a moist warm bread. Perhaps the thought that this might be her last meal made the food taste so good. She decided to try to pour some of the coffee, and spent some moments attempting to position herself so that the heavy dangling chain between her wrists wouldn't get in the way.

The door opened on silent hinges and Gina let out a scream, her chains jangling against the coffee pot, knocking the little lid off. "Well, good morning, Gina. I see you've found your breakfast. Excuse me, I didn't mean to startle you." The tall dark man walked in, smiling at Gina, who now sat huddled, her knees drawn up in an effort to hide her naked body.

"I was very rude last night, and I failed to introduce myself. My name is Frank." He waited, as if expecting her to respond with a "how do you do" or some other common formality. She simply stared at him, her large eyes widened by fear.

Frank seemed to barely notice that she was naked and in chains. It was as if they were at a tea party. He knelt near the tray and said solicitously, "Let me help you with that. Do you take sugar? Cream?" When Gina didn't answer his tone sharpened somewhat, "Cat got your tongue? Answer when I speak to you. Remember your place." This was no tea party.

Gina's voice cracked as she tried to answer. She began again, and managed, "Both, please." Deftly, Frank added the sugar and cream, still kneeling in an easy balance. He stirred the coffee and handed her the cup. She didn't dare refuse him. The coffee, like the muffin, was delicious, freshly brewed and flavorful. She sipped it gratefully, trying to keep her hands from trembling.

Because he seemed so civil, almost pleasant, she dared to say, "Look, my dad has money. If you want money, I promise I can get it for you. The church—"

He cut her off, laughing. "You ridiculous little girl! We don't want money! We have more than we need, don't you worry. We want you! I've already told you, you're our new toy! I know you aren't used to the idea yet, but this is your life now! There is no going back. Ever. Forget Dwayne, forget Mommy and Daddy. Gordon and I are your world now. Period. The sooner you get used to that, the better off you'll be."

"You won't get away with it! God will punish you!" Gina blurted this out, her voice pitched high.

Frank laughed again. "Well, that'll be our problem, not yours, wouldn't you agree?"

"My parents will find you. You'll go to jail—"

"Enough," his tone sharpened, and his eyes narrowed. "If they find us, we haven't done our jobs, and deserve to be found. Meanwhile, you belong to us. We've stolen you, if you like. You are our possession, to be used as we see fit. Now hush or I'll lose my temper. You wouldn't want that."

Frank crouched down next to Gina, who was hunched up near the top of her mattress. He reached out and touched the still damp fabric. "I see you had a little, uh, accident here," Frank nodded toward her damp bed. "Gordon does seem to have that effect on people. Let's get you cleaned up. He doesn't like his toys to be dirty. Oh no, we mustn't upset Gordon. That wouldn't do at all." Frank spoke in a light voice, as if he were talking about the weather or someone's grandmother. Just the mention of Gordon's name brought back his stern closed face, the slate gray eyes looking through her as if she didn't exist, or worse, that her existence was an affront to him.

The coffee had turned to mud in her mouth. Gina set the cup down and tried to cover herself again, shivering. "Had enough? That's all right. I won't take your loss of appetite personally, though I made those muffins just for you. Looks like you could lose a few pounds anyway, am I right, Gina?" Gina blushed crimson, outraged and humiliated that he considered her fat and had said so. Dwayne liked her the way she was; he assured her it was feminine and pleasing. She had believed him; her pleasure in sweets also persuading her that nothing need change.

"Well, not to worry. We'll make sure you get your exercise. But first we better get you cleaned up! Gordon is very fussy about hygiene. He's going to want you fresh and clean for his games. First, I'm going to take off your cuffs, but don't even think about doing something stupid like trying to get away. Gordon and I are both very strong, and we live miles and miles away from anywhere." As he spoke, Frank used a little key he removed from a chain around his neck. Gina rubbed her wrists as Frank held out his hand to her. "Up you get!" A very reluctant Gina took the offered hand, not daring to refuse.

He led her from the mirrored room, down a hallway to a bathroom. The room was colder than the one she had been confined in. Gina shivered, crossing her arms over her bare breasts. Frank pointed to the toilet. "Need to go?" Gina shook her head, though she did. There was no way she was going to pee in front of this man.

"Suit yourself, but I'd better warn you, if you piss in your bed again, you're going to be punished. If you want to hold it in, make sure you do it more effectively than last time!" He grinned as he watched Gina blush and duck her head. He led her to the shower, and turned on the water.

"Cold shower, I'm afraid. You'll have to earn a hot one. And you've certainly done nothing yet to earn that!" Frank pushed Gina until she stepped into the icy spray of water. She gasped and tried to back out.

"Stay in, Gina. Stay in or I'll make sure you do." The threat was vague, but enough for the poor girl to do as she was told. She stood miserably under the spray. Frank took the soap and began to rub her body with it, lathering it up. "Hands behind your head, and feet apart," he commanded. Gina assumed the required position, her teeth chattering from cold, her face burning with shame.

Frank lathered her efficiently, only lingering a moment over her pussy and nipples. He even washed her hair for her, and then had her rinse. He took her hand, helping her out of the tub and then roughly but efficiently dried her with a large soft towel. Her thick dark hair hung wetly down her back as he led her back to her mirrored prison.

It was warmer in there, and though Gina was still shivering from the cold shower, she was grateful for that small favor. The mattress was gone, leaving only the bare room, with several large and ominous looking hooks placed strategically on the floor and in the ceiling. Everywhere Gina saw her own naked form, reflected *ad infinitum* in the mirrored walls. She looked down, embarrassed anew.

Frank left her for a moment, and returned with a large box he set noisily on the floor. "Kneel," he commanded, pointing at his feet. Gina knelt, curling up as if she could disappear. "Hands out in front of you, forehead touching the floor, ass up high." As Frank spoke, he pulled and pushed Gina into the desired position, and then deftly attached leather cuffs to her wrists and ankles, and a large belt around her waist. He took chains designed for the purpose, and secured her at the waist, wrists and ankles to the hooks in the floor so that she was bound into position, unable to move. And there he left her.

• • •

Minutes passed that seemed like hours. Gina couldn't stop trembling. He hadn't killed her; that was something. She was still alive, and must thank God for that. This was a trial for her to endure. She didn't know why, but she knew she had to be strong and rely on her faith. It was hard to keep this in mind as she knelt, her head touching the cold wooden floor, her hands stretched out in front her, chained and held in place by the large hook embedded in the planks.

Her body shook and she couldn't seem to control it. She knew she must cut a ridiculous picture, her naked, rather large body displayed, ass forced up, legs splayed so that her bare sex was exposed. And she still had to pee. Tears seeped out of her eyes, tickling her nose, which had begun to run. Her legs were aching, tucked under her in this unaccustomed pose.

The sound of a key turning in the lock caused all thoughts of physical discomfort to fly from her head. Only the trembling was constant. The door opened slowly and Gordon came in, silent on bare feet. This time he was dressed in black jeans and no shirt. He carried something, a stick, in his hands. He set it down behind the prostrate woman and knelt near her.

"Good morning, cunt." His voice lacked the warmth, the humor, that Frank's had. The British tones were clipped and succinct. The word shocked Gina, causing her to blush, the heat flaming up her cheeks. A hand on her hair pulled up, hard. Gina gasped in pain.

"Speak when spoken to, cunt," he said calmly. "When I say good morning, cunt, you will answer, 'Good morning, master. I am your slave cunt.' Do you understand?" He spoke as if he were teaching her a simple phrase in a foreign language. He spoke slowly, clearly, with little inflection. Gordon pulled her hair harder, forcing her head up and back. Gina's eyes were squeezed shut and she began to whimper. "Now we'll try again, shall we?" he said, his voice low.

"Please," she began to beg. "Please, please don't do this. Please—"
He slapped her hard and let go of her hair.

"You are very stupid, aren't you, Gina? You can't follow the simplest command. Luckily, I have plenty of time. You certainly aren't going anywhere. So we'll start again. But first, a little punishment to help you remember to obey. I'm going to mark you with my favorite cane. It's a very effective little instrument favored in Thailand."

Gordon took the thin supple rod from the floor behind Gina. He brought it around to her face. "Open your eyes, cunt. This little cane may not look like much, but it will teach you your manners. Each time I use it on you, I will expect you to kiss it—a thank-you for being taught a lesson you will no doubt richly deserve. You may choose this time— a kiss before, or a kiss after. Which is it to be, cunt?"

Gina was crying in earnest now, her eyes and nose streaming. Gordon seemed entirely unconcerned. "I'll take your continued refusal to answer as meaning you'll kiss it after it kisses you." His mouth was a tight smile; his eyes glittered hard and bright. Going behind the naked young women, he bent and brought the thin cane down, hard, against her virgin flesh.

Gina yowled, the pain like a searing line of fire across her ass. Gordon watched the welt rise, turning from a fine white line to fiery red. Satisfied, he walked around the prostrate, bound girl and held the rod in front of her face. Her will broken, Gina forced her lips into a pucker and kissed the cane. Gordon nodded, looking satisfied. "Now. Good morning, cunt."

"G-good morning, um, master." She hiccupped and cried, "What else? God, I can't remember, please don't hurt me again!"

"'Good morning, master. I am your slave cunt.'"

"Good morning, master. I am your slave . . ." Her voice trailed to a whisper.

"I can't hear you, cunt. Say it again. Louder. If I can't hear it, I'll whip you again."

"Oh, please, oh no!" She sniffled loudly and began again, "Good morning, master. I am your slave c-cunt." The word actually hurt to say; she felt it stick in her throat like broken glass.

"Better. We'll work on it." He patted her wet head. "How ridiculous that words should embarrass you even more than your absurd position there on the ground. Your cunt is exposed. Your nasty, hairy, little twat cunt is right there. I'm looking at it, cunt. It's probably dry as a bone. Is it, Gina? Is your cunt dry as a bone? Tell me your cunt is dry as a bone, cunt."

A small sob. Gordon whooshed the cane through the air and she panted, "I don't know! Please, I don't know! I don't know what you want!" She screamed as bamboo hit flesh.

Ignoring her whimpering, Gordon said, "You don't know. Fair enough. I'll tell you." Turning, he straddled Gina's back, so that he was facing her ass. She gasped under his weight. Reaching under her, he pressed his hard finger into her pussy. Gina cried and tried to move away, but she was held fast in her chains.

"As I suspected. Dry. Nervous little Nellie. That's what we should call you. I'm going to teach you a lot of things, girl. One of them is that it's rude to be dry in front of your master. But since you are a new student, we will let it pass. Frank will teach you how to be wet. Much more his department. I—" He paused for effect. "—will make sure the lesson is learned." He stood up, and Gina sighed with relief as his weight was lifted from her. She longed to move; to close her legs, to escape.

"You will have your first lesson today. I am going to teach you about pain. You probably think you can't tolerate very much. I'm going to teach you that you can. But first Frank is going to teach you about pleasure." Without another word or glance at Gina, Gordon was gone. *Praise God*, she thought.

Several minutes later, though it felt like hours, Gina heard, "Hello, dear one. Gordon was not impressed, I'm afraid." Frank came in, smiling, and Gina realized with a small shock she was actually glad to see him, compared to Gordon at any rate. He seemed to be bustling about, but after a few minutes, amazingly, he began unlocking her chains! She didn't dare look around, but she felt him releasing the lock that held her leg chains in place. Then he came around and released her wrists. Gina still didn't dare to move. The burning marks from the cane reminded her to be still. Frank gently rolled her over, and Gina realized her arms and legs were asleep.

He had rolled her onto a soft pallet of cotton bedding he had placed next to her. She lay inert as he gently massaged her legs and arms, bringing the blood back with tingling but welcome relief. "Now Gina, listen carefully. I'm going to explain some things to you. Some things that might make it easier for you to get along here. Gordon says I don't need to explain anything to the toys, but I find it makes for an easier transition.

"First, as you may have gathered, Gordon is the boss here. I don't work for him exactly. You might say I belong to him. Much as you do, though you don't know it yet. I'm his boy; you're his toy." Frank grinned, his eyes twinkling, a faint flush on his cheeks. Gina stared at him uncomprehendingly.

"He's gay, stupid," Frank said, exasperated. Gina looked horrified, her Christian sensibilities offended anew. "Oh stop," Frank said, irritated. "Don't worry, I like girls. I just happen to like boys, too, and Frank is quite exciting, once you understand how he operates. You could really have a lot of fun, Gina, if you'd just drop the whole outraged religious kick.

"But anyway, here's the thing. Gordon likes boys, and he likes them without hair. He likes girls, too, to play with, just not as lovers. One reason we picked you is your tits aren't too big. He can't stand big old saggy boobs getting in the way of everything. You are kind of heavy, but he likes a big ass, and we see lots of potential in you, once we get you into shape. But the first thing we have to do is get all this hair off you. You can keep the hair on your head, he likes to use it when he's torturing you." A small gasp escaped from Gina's open mouth and she bit her lips.

"But the rest of it has to go. I'm going to bring you a snack, and then we'll go to the bathroom. I'm going to use warm water, only because it'll give us a closer shave. Don't think you've earned hot water yet, because you haven't. Now, you just relax a little and I'll be back in a flash. Your diet starts today."

He whirled out of the room, humming a tune as if he had no care in the world. He had kidnapped and was planning on keeping a woman captive, and he was singing! She was almost more frightened by his breezy confiding ways; his offhand manner was chilling, given the circumstances. At least Gordon played the part of villain as she would expect. What was she to make of Frank?

Gina closed her eyes, and images of her parents, who must be worried sick over her absence, and of Dwayne, her darling Dwayne, made the tears flow again. She wiped her nose across the back of her hand and then curled into a fetal position, her eyes tightly closed. A few minutes later Frank returned with a bowl of broth and some carrot sticks. Gina drank the hot liquid gratefully, and munched on the sticks. When she was done, she felt almost as hungry as before. "Had enough?" Frank smiled at her.

"Well, to tell you the truth," Gina began, but Frank put his finger to her lips.

"Not another word, Gina. You're on a diet now. You'll thank me later, believe me. You have a gorgeous body hiding inside that chubby exterior." Gina flushed angrily, but Frank went on. "I know what will distract you from your hunger. We'll go shave all that nasty girl hair off you and make you smooth as a baby. We'll be doing it every morning as part of your *toilette*," he said, giving the word its French pronunciation.

He held his hand out and Gina had no choice but to take it. He led her again out the door of her prison and along to the bathroom. This time when he pointed to the toilet, she sat, knowing if she did not, she would definitely have another accident.

Frank watched her, his face amused, as she blushed a hot red and was unable for a moment to urinate. But need overcame modesty and soon a steady hot stream splashed into the toilet, to Gina's great embarrassment and relief. Frank had her kneel on the bath mat while he ran the warm water into the tub. When he added something from a pretty glass bottle, the room filled with a lovely scent of sandalwood and a hint of lavender.

"Get in," he instructed, and she did. What a lovely feeling, sinking into the hot, sweetly-scented water. Her bottom hurt from the cane beating. The hot water soothed her and she relaxed slightly, actually allowing a little sigh of pleasure to escape. Frank seemed pleased. He began gently to soap her body, and then, using a small china pitcher, he rinsed her with the bath water.

Taking a small vial he said, "This is a special oil, very nice for shaving. It'll keep your skin baby soft. You really do have lovely skin, Gina. Did you know that?" Gina didn't know it. She was not at all used to compliments, but all the same, in some secret part of her, she was pleased by the remark.

"Now stay very still, and do as you're told, and things will go great. We don't want any nicks whatsoever, so make sure you obey me, do you understand? The only marks Gordon will want to see are the ones he makes on you himself." Gina shivered at his remark, and then her eyes grew round as he brought out a large and heavy looking old fashioned razor. He had her raise first one leg and then the other. His strokes were sure and smooth, and in no time he was done. Next her underarms, which caused a bit more trouble, because Gina was ticklish, and also mortified that he should be touching her so intimately. But she withstood it, and soon he was done.

"Now out of the bath with you. I want to shave your pussy while you sit on the counter. It's too hard to do in the tub."

"Oh, God. Please don't do that. I couldn't stand it. I'm begging you . . ." He cut her off gently.

"Now, now, Gina. You know the rules. Our master Gordon doesn't like hair. Especially nasty hairy little twats, as he calls them. It isn't up to me and it certainly isn't up to you. Cooperate or I'll have to call Gordon in to do it, and believe me, he doesn't mind a bit of blood at all."

Gina paled and felt herself swaying, her head light at the thought of her own blood, especially down there! Obediently she climbed from the tub and stood numbly as Frank toweled her dry. He set a fresh towel on the counter and pointed, waiting for her to hoist herself up.

"Good. Now spread your legs. Oh stop it, I've seen you naked for hours now. Please do get over this modesty thing! It's becoming really tedious." He smacked sharply at her thighs, and Gina reluctantly spread them a few inches. Setting down the razor, Frank used his own hands to push her legs far apart. "Now. Don't you dare close them or I'll tie your legs open. Do you understand?"

Gina had her eyes shut tight, but she kept her legs apart. First Frank used a small pair of barber's scissors, cutting away as much of the curls as he could. Gina tried to stay very still, frightened by the sharp cold blades so near her tender parts. Satisfied he had done all he could with the scissors, Frank lay them aside.

Gina felt the soft warm oil as he squirted some on his hand and rubbed it gently across her labia. It was a peculiar sensation; a nice one even, if she could have admitted this. Having been taught that to touch yourself is a sin, Gina had never done so. The sensation he was creating was a new one. She felt an odd mix of shame and pleasure, and longed to close her legs, but she didn't dare.

Frank was observant, and he noticed the sudden intake of breath, the small sigh that followed as he massaged her pussy lips, grazing over the clit. *The virgin isn't a total lost cause*, he thought gleefully. His fingers lingered longer than necessary as he watched the confusion and pleasure rushing across her open features, and her skin flushed a pleasing pink.

Deciding she'd had enough, he stopped suddenly, and Gina's eyes flew open as she bit her bottom lip, looking away as he laughed. He didn't say anything though, and she was grateful for that. The cool metal of the blade grazed her skin, gently removing the remaining hair. He passed the razor over and over her mons until he seemed satisfied at last that she would pass Gordon's strict muster. Finally he soothed some ointment over the area to heal any possible irritation.

"Okay, get down. It's almost time." For what she didn't know, but her heart constricted with fear at the remark. He had said she was being groomed for Gordon, for the master. The *master*! That made her a *slave*! Not just a hostage, but a slave, with the servitude and obedience that implied.

Frank led her back to her mirrored prison. Without speaking he led her to the center of the room. He lifted her arms over her head, securing her as she had been when Gordon whipped her. Gina began to thrash in panic. "Please! I can't! Please!"

Frank stopped her by placing his fingers gently against her mouth. "Hush, little one. No one is going to whip you. At least not at the moment." His eyes crinkled sardonically. "Just relax and take a look in the mirror." Gina, instead, looked down at the floor, the familiar feeling of shame at her nakedness flooding her anew. She didn't want to look. But Frank lifted her face, forcing her to see the image in the mirror. There she was, long dark hair curling prettily as it dried. Her cheeks were flushed and her eyes were dark. Her breasts looked perky and high, with her arms extended above her head. Her eyes were drawn to her bare pussy, the naked little cleft nestled between her thighs.

With a kick at her ankles, Frank forced Gina to spread her legs. The labia were pooching now, visible without the cover of curls. Gina felt sick with embarrassment. She had never seen her own body so denuded, so truly bare. Frank was also studying her critically. "We'll get you in shape. I think we'll start today with your exercise routine. And I'll cook for you. No more midnight hot cocoa and cookies for you, my love." He laughed and Gina was flustered, wondering how he knew that was her favorite time for a snack.

She wished she could lower her arms, cover her bare body, but of course she could not. Frank began to walk around her, so close she could smell his breath, which smelled sweet, like spearmint. "Now listen well, my pet," he murmured. "As of this moment your training truly begins. Gordon and I each have our roles as your teachers. While he is your stern taskmaster, which is a part he truly enjoys, I prefer a gentler touch. I will teach you through your body, through pleasure as well as pain."

As he spoke, he moved very close to her, so that they were standing face to face. She was glad the image of her plump naked form was blocked by his tall lean one. Her heart was hammering in her chest, but she didn't feel the abject terror she had felt when in this position before; when Gordon was caning her virgin flesh. Frank ducked his head so that he was nuzzling her neck, planting a series of tiny kisses on her skin. It tickled slightly and Gina shifted, an odd tension in her groin.

His head ducked further, tracing the gentle curve of her right breast, his lips moving with rapid little kisses down to her nipple. She felt an electric jolt shoot through her when his mouth reached the nipple. She felt it tighten, as if it were straining toward him. She had had this sensation before, when Dwayne was especially ardent in his kisses, but he had certainly never kissed her there!

Gina knew she should protest; resist. But really, what was the point? How ridiculous to try to voice her fundamentalist opinions about the female body as something strictly off limits until marriage, and even then only for procreation. She had no choice now. And words might only anger her captor, making him forget kisses in favor of something far worse.

As his mouth sought and found her second nipple, a little sigh, the tiniest of sighs, escaped Gina's lips, as her eyes fluttered closed. Her worried mind clicked off as, exhausted with the fears and tensions of these past two days, she succumbed to physical sensation at last.

Frank felt her relax; felt the tension lessen in her body. He smiled slightly, very pleased at her reaction. Kneeling, he let his mouth trail down between her breasts, down her belly to the plump little mons, bare as a baby's. Gina's legs were still spread, and Frank placed an index finger on either outer labia, spreading her pussy slightly.

Gina's eyes flew open and she jumped back, letting out a little scream. "Hush," Frank murmured, "hush. I won't hurt you. I know you're a virgin, Gina. I also imagine that you've never discovered your own body. Well, it's high time you did, and I'm going to help you do it. You really have no choice in the matter, Gina. No choice at all."

No choice at all. No choice at all. It became a mantra in her head as Frank spread her lips farther. No choice in the matter as she felt his warm wet tongue dart between the folds. No choice in the matter as she felt a strange hot liquid pleasure begin to build inside of her as his tongue swirled across her little nubbin. No choice in the matter. No choice at all.

And then even the words were obliterated, drowned out by pure sensation, pure pleasure. She didn't even flinch as he slid a finger into her pussy, which was wet and slippery now with his kisses and with her own juices. The pleasure continued to mount until Gina moaned, and then cried out, her body jerking with spasms of pleasure. Frank held each hip with his large hands, keeping her still as he continued to suckle and kiss her until she was truly spent.

Gina sagged in her chains; she would have fallen if she hadn't been tethered there. Frank stood up, his face glistening with her juices. The room was ripe with the scent of sex. Gina's face was flushed and her neck and chest were mottled from the rush of blood throughout her body as she orgasmed.

Frank unlocked the cuffs and supported her as Gina slid to the ground. He held her head on his lap while she recovered. The sensation was completely new to her, and she felt totally spent. When her breathing slowed and he no longer felt her heart pounding against him, he said, "That was the beginning, Gina. Just the beginning. I am going to claim you so completely you will live for my touch."

Gina felt the gentle throb in her pussy. A quiet sense of euphoria totally overtook the usual feeling of shame and guilt when she and Dwayne exchanged stolen fumbling kisses in his car. Something had started in Gina as irresistible as the first lick of a flame around a match. Gina believed what Frank said. And she realized it wasn't a threat, but a promise.

• • •

Frank left Gina sleeping, but she was instantly awake when Gordon entered, carrying a large multi-tressed whip. He didn't speak to her, but hauled her up roughly and secured her leather cuffed wrists to a chain and then to the ceiling, leaving her straining on tiptoe.

Taking a rubber ball gag from his bag of tricks, Gordon forced Gina's mouth open and buckled it behind her head. Gina was horrified at the image of herself in the mirrors, with the bright red ball and eyes wide in fear. She couldn't make a sound, as the ball pushed her tongue back in her throat.

Gordon came close and attached a small alligator clip to each nipple. The clips were connected by a silver chain. As the teeth bit into Gina's tender nipples, she struggled violently, a muffled cry issuing from behind the rubber ball rammed into her mouth. She was terrified that she was being cut, unaware that the clamps would do no permanent damage. She saw the chain swaying between her breasts, the clips pressing her nipples, reddened, flat between silver teeth.

Her head felt light and she might have fallen, but the chains that bound her kept her upright. No preamble, no explanation, and Gordon began to whip Gina's back, her ass, her thighs. His whipping was methodical and thorough. Soon every part of her back and ass was stinging, on fire. Then he moved to the front. Though not a tall man, he was very strong, and didn't seem at all exerted from the whipping, which had gone on for some minutes.

When the lash hit the clamps on her nipples, Gina screamed in agony and swayed, leaning hard into the chains, all her weight on her wrists. Her eyes rolled up and she sagged there. Gordon lowered the whip, studying her for a moment. His cock was pressing hard against his jeans, and he shifted it a little as he waited for her to come to.

A minute or so later the poor girl opened her eyes and, focusing on Gordon with his whip, she jerked back, as if she could somehow escape. But there was no escape. He had promised he would teach her about pain, and he made good on that promise. After thoroughly whipping her front, he removed the nipple clamps. As the blood rushed back, engorging the nipples, tears of pain sprang to Gina's eyes.

But she forgot this as he attached the wicked clips to her labia. The chain jangled and hit her thighs as she danced in pain, vainly trying to escape the whipping that continued without mercy. Finally, Gordon seemed satisfied. He let Gina down, and she lay where she fell, completely immobile, as if dead.

Gordon felt a flash of concern; had he gone too far? But as he unbuckled the ball gag and removed the clamps from her pussy, she began to cry and he knew she would be fine. It was when they turned "zombie" that he had to worry. It wouldn't do to frighten them so badly they lost their wits. He liked his slaves alert and completely aware of what was happening to them. Still without speaking to her, Gordon kissed the top of Gina's head, and went to find Frank so he could make use of this delicious hard on.

Chapter 3

A LESSON IN MODESTY

Gina was asleep on the mattress—there was little else to do—when the door opened and she realized with a little shock that she actually wanted to see Frank. It was certainly better than being alone, she told herself as an excuse. She had come to realize that Gordon must work during the day, because she saw him only after her third meal. She measured time by her meals, having no watch or clock to rely upon, and no window. Frank was her daily and constant companion, and as odd as it seemed, she almost regarded him as a friend.

But it wasn't Frank. It was Gordon. And he was carrying a large bag, which Gina was sure had horrible things in it. She sat up, instantly terrified. Gordon said, "Good afternoon, cunt. How are you?" Gina remembered her lessons as fear spurred her tongue.

"Good afternoon, master. I am your," she pause imperceptibly but forced herself to go on, "slave cunt." Gordon's mouth twisted slightly in an approximation of a smile.

"That you are, Gina. Good that you are starting to realize it. First of all, let's inspect Frank's handiwork today. Roll over on your back, arms behind your head, and legs spread." Reluctantly, but with the sharp memory of his cane fresh in her mind, Gina did as she was told. Gordon's eyes raked her form and his gaze was like heat running up and down her naked, bare body. Leaning toward her, he stroked her soft smooth skin, his fingers moving from her legs slowly up to her bare and spread pussy. Gina couldn't help but squeeze her eyes shut, but somehow she remained still. Fear of his wrath outweighed any modesty. After some moments, Gordon stood. He seemed satisfied, if no comment meant satisfaction.

Finally he said. "Okay, cunt girl. You can close your legs now. I've seen enough." Gratefully, Gina did so, also wrapping her arms around her torso in a protective gesture. Gordon ignored her. "Today I have devised a few tests for our mutual pleasure. Well, for my pleasure anyway. Frank and I have observed that you are excessively shy, modest to the point of absurdity. He likes to coax, but I prefer a more direct method. I am going to help you overcome your modesty. I will help you realize that your modesty is an affront to me; a personal affront. A good slave is completely immodest. That doesn't mean promiscuous; it means that you are completely open to your master on every level. It means that nothing, no matter how others might think it debases or humiliates you, is to be resisted if your master wants it done.

"Now," he went on calmly, enjoying the look of terror on her face, the fear in her round, dark eyes, "you seem to be excessively prudish, even for a virgin, and I imagine you are also very, shall we say, private, about your bodily functions. That won't do at all. When I'm done with you, you'll be able to piss in front of me, to move your bowels, to make yourself orgasm in whatever position I have you in and whenever I demand it, to lick me clean from head to toe, to swallow my semen and my urine, if that's what I want—"

Gordon broke off suddenly, realizing that the poor stupid cow had actually fainted again! He did seem to have that effect on the woman! It was getting tedious. However, Gordon was nothing if not prepared. He took a pitcher of ice water he had brought in with him and dumped it unceremoniously over Gina's face and chest.

Gina sputtered and shrieked, consciousness quickly regained. "Don't do that again," Gordon warned, as if she could control the waves of horror that had made her so dizzy she passed out. "Next time I'll bring you to with this." He withdrew a long-handled switchblade from his back pocket and Gina felt her breath catch in her throat. As he flicked the blade open, she gasped in fear. Again she felt the now familiar heaviness in her head, the dizziness and nausea, the slight ringing in her ears, and knew she could faint again, easily. But he had said she could control it, and she must.

She did. The dizziness receded as she focused on his shoes, which were rich chocolate brown leather boots, the outline of which she could see under his pants. "Better," he said as he walked around behind her.

He went over to the pile of things he had brought in with him and after a moment said, "Stand up." She did so. "Assume the position." She stood as he had instructed her earlier, with fingers laced behind her head, and legs spread smartly apart, like a soldier at ease.

"Here, drink this." She wasn't sure if she was supposed to move from *the position* but he seemed to want her to take it so she reached out for the glass. Snatching it out of her reach, Gordon pursed his lips and said, "That was a test. You failed. I will remember your failure and punish you for it, rest assured. Next time, ask first. You will say, 'Please sir, may I move out of position?'"

Gina colored, angry that he had baited her this way, but of course not daring to voice it. Instead, she nodded and whispered, "I'm sorry, sir," and then, "Please, sir, may I move out of position?" He nodded, and Gina reached a trembling hand out for the offered glass.

It was bubbly and smelled like alcohol, something she never drank. "It's champagne. It'll help you for a task I have in mind later. Drink it. It won't send you to hell, I promise." Stung by his slur, she tasted it. It really was quite good! It was dry and wet all at once, and fizzy and sweet, but tart. Hard to describe, but very good. She sipped again. Before she realized it, the glass was empty.

"More?" asked her host, if you could call him that. Gina held out her glass as a silent yes and he filled it, smiling with amusement. Gina drained it quickly and suddenly felt the oddest sensation in her head. She was dizzy again! Not the sick, nauseated dizzy she felt when fear had made her faint, but a different kind of silly dizzy! Unconsciously she smiled, which changed her face from merely pretty to actually beautiful. Her grandmother used to say that when Gina smiled it was like an angel jumped inside her for a minute. She fairly sparkled.

Even though his sexual tastes leaned quite the other way, Gordon could appreciate her beauty, and did so, really for the first time. Up until now he hadn't seen past the plump body, the dark thick tangle of hair, the very "femaleness" of her which held no allure for him at all. But now he saw something which ignited something physical in him, something almost sexual. He wanted to see her smile again.

"Did you like that, Gina? That's a really fine champagne. I only drink the best. Have you ever had champagne before?"

"No, sir," Gina answered, sitting down suddenly without permission. "I've never had any alcohol at all, sir. My parents didn't think I should drink till I got married, and then maybe some wine on our anniversary, like they do."

Gordon let it pass that she was now sitting, legs tucked under her, without permission. He realized she was drunk and was actually charmed by her total innocence. "Would you like some more?"

"Please." She smiled again, more a grin than a smile, but she still looked beatific. He poured and watched her drink again. Realizing she'd be good for nothing if he gave her any more, he put the bottle down. He ordered her to get up, which Gina did, stumbling a little as the alcohol upset her equilibrium.

"Now," Gordon spoke briskly as he brought over a large metal bowl, "lesson number one in modesty. I want you to squat over this bowl and urinate into it." Gina looked up at him, confused. She knew she must be drunk, but found the feeling quite pleasant. The wild edge of terror that had pressed in on her since her abduction was somehow blunted by the champagne. She tried to focus on Gordon. Surely she had misunderstood him.

Again he said, his tone sharp, "Get up and do as you're told." Awkwardly Gina got to her feet. She swayed a bit, then stood with a leg over either side of the bowl. Embarrassment began to outweigh the pleasant high from the alcohol. This horrible man wanted her to pee in front of him! She really did have to go, now that she thought of it. It had been hours since they had let her use the toilet, and the champagne had certainly made it worse!

Gina, naked and already humiliated in front of this cold, strange man, knew she had better obey. She knelt, squatting over the bowl, and tried to pee. Her natural shyness kept her from complying at first, but then the sound of liquid hitting the bowl, and the warm pungent smell of urine, made it clear she had complied with his odd demand. Gina stayed crouching, wondering what to do now. Gordon didn't seem to be offering her any toilet paper. Her legs were cramping and she felt ridiculous and ashamed huddled over a bowl of her own urine!

Gordon, as usual, seemed completely unconcerned or unaware of her discomfiture. "Get up."

"Please, sir. Um, excuse me?"

"What?"

"May I speak, sir?"

She was learning at last the language of a slave. Gordon smiled but only said, "Yes."

"Um, toilet paper? I need some."

"No you don't."

"But—"

"I said you don't. End of discussion. Stand up. You did passably well. Now you will be punished." Punished! But she had done as he asked. Gina felt a panic rise in her. Any trace of euphoria from the champagne was squelched under the terror of a promised punishment. She barely registered the little droplets of urine that rolled down her inner thighs as she stood.

"You passed this test of modesty, but you have forgotten your earlier transgression, that of moving out of position without permission. You will be punished for that, and also because it pleases me to punish you. I like the way you quiver when I beat you. Today I think we'll try something new. I'm going to tie you up like the fat little calf you are, and then watch you squirm away from my whip."

Gina was trembling, hugging her naked body. She considered for a moment trying to fight him. Somehow pushing him aside, getting away, running through the door which he had not locked. But he was standing between her and that door. She looked at his strongly muscled chest and arms, and at the rope he was uncoiling. She stayed motionless, feeling her momentary courage evaporate as he approached her.

"Kneel." She collapsed, kneeling at his feet. Gordon coiled the thin supple rope around the poor naked girl, trussing her arms behind her back, securing her at the elbows, knees and ankles, so that she fell onto her side, unable to balance. Around and around her body he looped the strong cords, until she was completely immobile; completely helpless.

Then the whipping began. He used the riding crop, smacking her exposed flesh in a rhythmic tattoo. He started lightly, smacking her ass and thighs, which were exposed through the fine ropes coiling around her. He couldn't get a proper smack at her pussy, and so contented himself with smacking her ass until it was a lovely rosy red, which looked especially nice against the white rope. Coming around to her front, he playfully smacked her tits. She couldn't move at all to block the blows. Squeezing her eyes tight, she gave a tiny squeal with each blow. Gordon's cock hardened painfully in his pants. When he hit her nipples, she screamed. He did it again and again, until the flesh was numb and she had subsided to a whimpering.

As she lay gasping and sweating, her body contorted in its ropes, Gordon approached with a small greased dildo. Aware of her still virgin state, he didn't want to tear his toy, his property. Not with this at any rate. Gina's eyes were closed, and she didn't open them as he loomed over her. He didn't speak or warn her of what was to come. Even tied as she was, when he knelt down, he could see her pussy peaking out between her legs. Gina jerked forward when she felt the hard unfamiliar object press against her virgin opening. Using one hand, Gordon spread her pussy lips, allowing easier access. Slowly but relentlessly he slipped the phallus into her body, violating her innocence with the greased plastic penis. Gina screamed as he pushed it in to the hilt. She continued screaming as he walked out the door, leaving her bound and alone in the room full of mirrors.

•••

When Frank found her, Gina lay still bound, perhaps asleep. She had pushed the offending dildo from her pussy, and it lay near her contorted and tied body. Upon closer inspection, Frank saw that she wasn't asleep; her eyes were open, but she showed little reaction when he crouched near her. Gina had screamed herself hoarse, finally subsiding, giving up, as she drifted in and out of consciousness.

The dildo had hurt her, but mostly it had scared her to have some- thing shoved into her like that. Her vaginal muscles had clamped down on the offending object, and thus had held it in place. As she rocked and moaned, the phallus moved gently inside her. When she had calmed and quieted, Gina realized with a shock that the feeling wasn't entirely unpleasant. In fact, it felt almost good, like some kind of massage from the inside out. She was confused by her feelings, and so she stopped thinking about it, just letting her body rock and move in such a way that the phallus shifted pleasantly inside of her.

As she relaxed, exhausted from struggling against her bonds, her vaginal muscles eased and the phallus slipped out. Gina was at once relieved and a little sorry. She mentally scolded herself, wondering what was happening to her. Now Frank was next to her, sitting cross-legged as he untied the knots that bound her. Those he couldn't undo, he cut with a sharp penknife he had brought for the purpose. Gina lay still, not looking at him or responding to his presence in any way. Once the ropes were off, Frank forced Gina's legs to uncurl. They were stiff and cramped from being bent under her for so long. Rolling her gently from her side to her back, he stretched her legs out slowly. When he saw the dildo lying nearby, still greasy from the jelly, he knew what Gordon must have done.

It was a small dildo, but to Gina it had probably felt huge. Was this why she was so quiet? He leaned down toward her face and whispered, "Gina? Are you okay?" She didn't answer, but he could see she had heard him. He considered a reprimand for her insubordination, her failure to answer when questioned, but decided against it.

Instead, he spread her legs slightly, and she offered no resistance. It was almost as if she had left her body for a while. He hoped she would come back, was sure she would, but meanwhile, he was curious. Using his index and middle fingers, Frank gently spread Gina's labia, while with the other hand he forced her thighs further apart. Still no protest. He licked a finger and slowly, carefully, inserted it into her pussy.

Finally a reaction, as Gina gasped, her voice still hoarse from screaming. Her body spasmed slightly in response to his invasion. Frank held her still, and kept his finger buried in the warm velvety tunnel. Slowly he began to move his finger till he felt a sweet wetness begin inside of her.

Though her mind had not allowed her to think about it, Gina's body remembered that first orgasm. Exhaustion had lowered Gina's defenses, and now she felt with her body, while her mind was shut down. There were literally no thoughts in her head. She gave herself over to sensation. It was so much easier than constantly fighting. And this sensation at least was pleasant. She liked his warm supple finger inside of her. It was much nicer than the thing Gordon had pressed into her.

He slowly moved the finger and withdrew it, only to move it up to her hardening clit. He circled the clit, the circle wide at first and then closing in on the sensitive engorged flesh. When he touched the hooded button, Gina moaned slightly but still did not move. She was like a great rag doll, inert and limp, naked on the floor. Frank's fingers slid back to her now slick opening, pressing in two this time. Using his thumb, he massaged her clit while finger fucking her, first slowly, and then with more intensity.

Gina's body began to move, to arch up into his hand. Her eyes were shut, lips apart, glistening as she licked them. Frank felt his cock harden and his own breath quicken with desire as he watched her respond. He wanted to fuck her, now. This minute. She was his naked slave, his toy for his use and pleasure. He could rape her; he could do whatever he wanted to her, as long as he left her available for Gordon.

Of course, Gordon had first claim on her cunt. He always used the slaves first, but quickly lost interest in the girls. Still, how would Gordon know if Frank fucked her first? She'd still be plenty tight, plenty new, after just one penetration. And Gordon wasn't even home. Frank could fuck her now and there was no one to stop him, certainly not Gina. And yet, despite his rock hard cock, he realized with some surprise that he didn't want to fuck her. Not yet. She was too new. She certainly wasn't ready yet. He wanted her to want it.

This was odd, this sudden consideration of a toy's feelings! He would have to think about this. But meanwhile, he liked how ardently she responded—this virginal little priss was pressing against him like any slut in heat. Her cheeks were flushing a pleasing pink, and her rose colored nipples were erect and straining from her soft white breasts.

Impulsively, Frank leaned over and kissed the hard little nipple of one breast, then the other. He suckled gently, and Gina, eyes still closed, moaned sweetly, thrusting herself against his mouth. He rubbed her pussy harder, alternating between finger fucking her and massaging her hard pleasure bud, now soaked with her own juices.

Her breathing was shallow, fast and jagged in her throat. He could feel her heart pounding on his cheek as he kissed and bit her nipples. Kneeling between her knees, he lowered his head till he was at her pussy, where he inhaled the sweet musky scent of her. He delicately licked her labia.

Frank had expected some protest at this point. He was certain oral sex was taboo in her religious code. But still no resistance was offered. He began to lick and nibble her labia and clit, while still keeping a finger or two embedded in her hot wet pussy. Gina was gasping, her voice cracked and low from her prior ordeal, but aching with passion.

Suddenly he felt her body stiffen and arch, and her cries escalated, her register high now, piercing. As she came, he felt her muscles clamp around his fingers, and her body jerked up against his mouth. Still he continued to gently kiss and tease her until the last spasm had subsided. Then he lay next to her, kissing her face.

Slowly Gina opened her eyes and looked at him, lying close to her on the floor. She looked so satisfied, like a baby that has had lots of delicious milk. As the sadist in him got the upper hand, Frank couldn't resist saying, "You'll have to be punished, you know." Gina's eyes widened in fear and surprise, but still she didn't speak.

"Yes," Frank went on, "you'll have to be punished for coming without permission. You know that's a rule, don't you? A slave must always ask first, because that body isn't yours, not any more. We own it. We use it however we want, and when we make you come, you have to ask permission to use our body. But maybe you did that on purpose, huh? Maybe you like to be punished now. Maybe it's getting under your skin, and you are becoming the pain/pleasure slut that lives inside each of us. I guess we'll find out, soon enough."

• • •

Days passed. It might have been weeks, as time lost its meaning for Gina. She had stopped believing that her death was imminent. Now, with the amazing capacity humans have for adapting, she simply got from day to day as best she could, avoiding beatings when possible, trying to learn what was expected and what was required of her. It could have been afternoon . . . probably was. Gina was in her most common position, though this time Frank had thoughtfully placed a pad beneath her knees. She was kneeling, hands tied loosely behind her back, hair pulled into a long ponytail behind her. Her mouth was wide open, and Frank was easing the tip of his very erect cock into it. She, of course, was naked.

Frank had unzipped his jeans, pulling out his cock for her, but otherwise had remained fully clothed. Except for the eyes squeezed shut, the face a study in distaste, Gina was behaving well, all things considered. Gordon would have probably whipped her for that expression, but Frank's approach was more subtle. He would teach her not only to behave as if she enjoyed what she was doing; he would actually teach her to love it. As the spongy tip of his penis touched her lower lip, Gina moved back slightly. At a reminder from Frank, she stilled and remained obediently in position.

Slowly Frank eased just the head into her mouth. "Lick it. Just around the head; see what the texture is like, the taste. Take your time." Eyes still squeezed comically shut, Gina's pink tongue licked the underside of the head, and then circled up to the top. Frank eased his cock just slightly further into her mouth. Soft lips closed lightly around it and Frank sighed with pleasure. "That's it," he urged. "Gently, slowly, you want to tease, to make the man want more; to make him beg for it."

Gina wasn't thinking at the moment. She had let her mind leave, as she was becoming adept at doing these days. Her body was here, and she wasn't being hurt or frightened, so she was able to obey his careful instruction. As long as she knelt here, learning to suck Frank's penis, no one would beat her, and hopefully she wouldn't have to see Gordon. She actually sort of liked the way Frank's penis was hard, but soft at the same time. The skin was smooth and silky over his rock hard erection. She continued to suckle and kiss the tip of his cock until Frank took her head in his hands and gently eased his cock further into her mouth.

Alarmed, Gina pulled back, but Frank held her still, admonishing,

"Now stop it, silly girl. It's still not even halfway in! I know you can do better than that! Gordon wanted to gag you with a penis gag overnight to desensitize you, but I told him that really wouldn't be necessary. I promised him I could teach you to suck a dick like a pro without it. Don't make a liar of me, slave girl, or you'll have to suffer, make no mistake."

Gina looked up at him, nodding slightly, fear in her face. She would try to obey him. Willing herself to relax, she allowed Frank to begin again, gently easing his shaft into her mouth. "Yes," he sighed, pleasure running through his body as her supple tongue began to move up and down his cock. "Slower, take it easy. Remember, it's a tease. The object is to make it last as long as possible; to draw out the pleasure until they can't take one more second."

They spent the better part of an hour working on Gina's technique. When he let her rest, Gina's jaw was aching and felt like it was coming unhinged. Frank still hadn't come, and he made it clear that this was just a break, not the end of the lesson. After having Gina do her daily exercise routine, he gave her some water and had her kneel again, ready for more advanced technique.

"Relax, look at me. Open your eyes. A man likes to see your eyes while you kiss him, and then you can close them when he closes his. Yes, oh, yes, that's very good." As Gina nibbled and suckled his hard smooth cock, Frank began slowly to press it further and further into her mouth, till the head was just touching the soft palate. Gina pulled away, gagging slightly.

"Shh," Frank whispered. "Just relax, you can do this. You've handled much more difficult tasks than an average sized dick!" He laughed, holding her head so she couldn't pull away again. Then slowly he pressed his cock back into her throat, ignoring her stifled protests. Gina gagged and thrashed, but Frank held her, unyielding until she stilled. His cock was blocking her windpipe and she was getting lightheaded from the lack of oxygen. As she relaxed, he loosened his grip and allowed his cock to slide back, letting her gasp for breath.

"We'll work on that, sweetheart. It takes a while to really let go and learn how to overcome that gag reflex. I know you can do it though. You've already shown great potential. I do believe that you have a knack for this! My, my, what would Daddy say about this, little girl?"

What indeed? Gina shuddered at the thought. What she was doing was clearly a sin in the eyes of her father, and until recently, in her own eyes as well. She wasn't saying it was okay, but Gina no longer arbitrarily insisted in her head that she was sinning and would go to hell for what was happening to her. There had to be a gray area, and she was definitely in it.

"Here's something that helped me when I was first learning. You practice with this; it helps you get used to something back there in your throat, but it's not so invasive as a dildo. Here, open up, come on, there's a girl." Frank had taken out a teaspoon. It was real silver and glinted in the fluorescent light. When Gina didn't immediately open her mouth, he gently smacked the bowl of the spoon against her lips, his foot tapping impatiently. Reluctantly, she opened her mouth, and Frank slid the spoon back till it touched her soft palette.

When he pushed it a little further, Gina gagged and pulled back. He held her by the back of the head, forcing her to stay still, and again eased the spoon in, sliding the bowl back into her throat. Tears reflexively sprang to Gina's eyes, but she could not get away from the strong man and she gave up, relaxing. He held the spoon in place for some moments longer and then said, "Much better. We'll make a suck slut out of you yet, my girl." He dropped the spoon next to the kneeling woman and again positioned himself in front of her, cock still erect and ready.

This time he eased his cock in slowly till it was again lodged in her throat. Gina stayed still and didn't gag or struggle. Frank began to move back and forth, his hips gently thrusting so that his cock slid in and out of her throat, creating an exquisite friction.

For several minutes he used her, fucking her face. "Oh, God!" he cried out suddenly, and withdrew entirely, spurting his load over Gina's face and breasts. She yelped in surprise and horror, as he splattered her with a hot sticky goo. Frank sighed happily, and then, noticing Gina's reaction, he laughed, amused by her agitation over a little cum.

Carefully he released her wrists from behind her back, and pulled back the hair that had come loose from her ponytail. Kissing her on the cheek he said, "Clean up, sugar, we're not done yet." He tossed her a soft cloth and while she was cleaning herself, he lay down on her mattress. "Come over here. Now you have a harder job. You have to arouse me, make me hard and then make me come again. And not only that, but you are going to swallow it this time when I come."

Gina was shaking her head; she would not swallow that nasty gray goo! She would rather be whipped. She didn't say anything though, as she crawled to her master. He hadn't noticed the head shake, as he was busy slipping entirely out of his jeans to allow her better access. Gina liked to look at his body. She silently admired the long firm muscles of his well-shaped arms and legs. She liked the curly line of hair from his belly button to his pubic bone. She liked his olive-toned skin and the little hollows below his hips.

His cock was lying semi-erect, looking small now in its little nest of pubic curls. Gina stared at it uncertainly. What should she do? As if she had spoken aloud, Frank said, "Take it in your hand, gently. Like it's a delicate piece of china. There's time for a firmer grip later, but now you are going to tease it to life. You are going to give it butterfly wing kisses with your fingers and your mouth. You will slip in the side door, if you will, slide past the gate, when all defenses are down.

He stopped talking, because she was doing as he had instructed, and she did indeed have a natural talent. Her fingers were long and cool against his flesh, and her mouth was hot and wet. She knelt over him, slowly teasing his cock into a full erection again. This time she had the use of her hands, and he didn't control her movements. She was more relaxed as a result, and was able to take him further into her throat without gagging.

She liked the woodsy, musky scent of him, and she took a certain pride in getting his flaccid penis fully erect. It was harder to take into her throat when it was so big, but she did the best she could, moving up and down the shaft, her mouth followed by her deft fingers. When she gently cupped the heavy balls, Frank arched back with pleasure and shuddered. He was deep in her throat when this happened, but she pulled back in a panic, not wanting his sticky emission on her tongue. As a result, instead of it sliding harmlessly down her throat, the cum squirted in her mouth and dribbled down her chin onto her breasts. Gina gagged and shuddered, coughing and crying.

Frank was annoyed. "Stupid girl. If you'd just stayed still you wouldn't have even tasted it! Now stop it; it isn't that bad! Jesus, you'd think I'd pissed in your mouth for God's sake. Stop it!" Gina continued to sputter, wiping her face on the sheet and making a terrible expression. As the endorphins of pleasure began to ebb, Frank became increasingly annoyed.

"Okay, that's it, Gina. You disobeyed by pulling away, and then you make this ridiculous display. I know I usually save the punishment for Gordon, but this is just too much. Get over here. I'm going to give you a good old fashioned spanking. Come on. Over my knee. Now!" His voice was no longer playful, and there was a cruel glint in his eye.

Gina crawled hesitantly over to him. "Please," she implored. "I'm sorry, I just wasn't expecting it. It's so gross and—"

"Enough!" He cut her off. "You're only making it worse by talking like that. Now, you've earned a spanking and you're going to get one. Get your ass over here now, Gina." His tone was cold and Gina felt her stomach tighten with fear. But she obeyed, knowing it would be worse for her if she didn't. She draped herself carefully over Frank's knees. He was sitting up on her mattress, and as she lay across him, he put a strong hand on her neck to keep her still.

"Now, don't struggle, don't cry out. Lie here and take it. You know damn well you deserve it." With that, he began to slap her ample ass. Even as she had begun to lose weight and tone up, the shapely globes of her bottom were still large and round, perfect for a really good spanking. Frank was secretly delighted at this opportunity to smack her luscious bottom until it turned cherry red.

And that's what he did, hitting first one cheek and then the other. Gina was quiet at first, but as the blows continued to fall and her skin turned to fire, she started to squirm and cry out. "Be still!" he hissed at her, punctuating the words with an especially hard smack on her tender flesh. He liked to watch the ass cheeks jiggle with each blow. The creamy white skin was flushing nicely with his hand print showing white for a second before it faded to hot pink.

Gina was crying now, little hiccupping mews of pain, until Frank's hand was tired, and he let her up. She rolled away from him, her hands massaging the burning flesh of her ass. Seeing her tear streaked face, Frank snapped out of whatever dominant space he had been in and reverted to the caretaker he usually was.

"Hush now, sweetheart. It's all over. You took your punishment well, and you know you needed it. If I don't knock that disobedience out of you, Gordon will do it. Better me than him. You know that." Wiping away a tear, he smiled, and then said, "Here, honey. Just lay on your tummy and I'll fix you right up."

He left the room for a moment and returned with the soothing balm he used on her skin after shaving her pussy every morning. Now he massaged it gently into the abraded mottled flesh of her ass. His fingers hurt her even as they soothed, but Gina lay still, knowing the cream would speed healing. She relaxed, giving in to Frank's smooth fingers over her ass and thighs. Without knowing it, she slept, and Frank slipped out to prepare for his master's return.

Chapter 4

METAMORPHOSIS

Time lost meaning for Gina. No sunlight, no stars, no way to mark the passage of the hours, the days. Her life was spent waiting, sleeping, training, suffering, and waiting again, with time measured by visits from her jailers and then blessed release. When the knob turned, the key causing the lock to click and scrape open, Gina's heart would pound while she waited to see who had come for her. Gordon meant fear and pain, though he did show an occasional spark of tenderness. Frank was more gentle. He still hurt her sometimes, but it was in a way that was increasingly confusing. The sweet rush of orgasm would be marred by a sudden smack or pull of her hair that made Gina's response uncertain. Pleasure and pain sometimes combined in a way that she didn't understand. Her body, it seemed, was being rewired to associate pleasure and suffering, agony and ecstasy.

Time was also measured by meals, soups and fruit mostly, which always left Gina hungry for more. But Frank never asked her if she wanted more, and she didn't dare ask for it. She was secretly pleased at the idea that she might lose some weight. She had tried a few half-hearted diets before, but Dwayne had pretty much assuaged any fears as to her desirability. He assured her he liked her that way, and didn't want her to change. It occurred to her for the first time that maybe he wanted her a bit plump so she would be less attractive to other men.

In her somber modest clothing, with her unruly hair usually pulled back in a tight bun, and no makeup, Gina hadn't exactly had to fend off the few men she came into contact with. Dwayne himself was rather heavy set, or big boned, as he liked to say. He would probably end up fat like his father, old at forty-two, spending his Sunday mornings in church and afternoons on the couch watching football, while his timid wife brought him beer and chips, making sure both were in plentiful supply. Gina felt guilty and surprised that she would have such thoughts. She had always considered herself a very loyal person. She was beginning, for the first time, to question some aspects of her life. For a young woman not at all used to introspection, her enforced leisure time gave her ample opportunity.

Frank had also put Gina on an exercise regime, one which humiliated her terribly, since it was done with her still completely naked and in front of those horrible mirrors. He would lead her through aerobic exercises and then have her ride an exercycle till the sweat poured between her breasts, and she soaked the plastic seat. He was like her trainer, her coach, at these times. It was as if they were preparing for some type of sporting event. He would stand near her, counting, encouraging, offering her a drink of water from the sipper cup he kept handy.

She was always slightly hungry, so she barely noticed it anymore. She did notice her body, the way it was slimming and changing. And her face was thinning as well, revealing cheekbones and setting off her full mouth and large eyes. As Gina's body began to strengthen and she built up a little stamina, she began to almost look forward to their sessions. At least no one was whipping her, or shaving her, or forcing her into uncomfortable positions. And when it was over, she was allowed to shower, with hot water! Gina had come to appreciate the slightest reward, and hot water was a big one. When she was free, she used to hurry in and out of the shower, washing quickly and efficiently, never lingering. Now she appreciated the delicious stream of liquid heat coursing over her. Sometimes it would sting where she had been freshly whipped, but even that felt good and ultimately soothed her.

Because so much attention had now been paid to her body, though most of it was what she would consider negative attention, she was much more self-aware. She would notice now, for the first time in her life, how the water felt cascading down her breasts, splashing on and stimulating her nipples. Sometimes as she was washing herself, her fingers would brush her clit, and she'd feel arousal, something that had never happened to her before. If Frank hadn't been right there in the bathroom, watching her shower, she might have let her fingers linger at her bare pussy. She told herself she was just washing carefully, because

Frank wanted her clean, but if she had probed her own motives, she would have known otherwise.

She even found herself wondering what it would be like to be fucked by Frank. Neither of them had used her in that way, and while she had been relieved and thanked God for it, sometimes now she actually found herself wondering why not. Was she so repulsive to them? Gordon she understood, but Frank? Why didn't he have sex with her? Did he think she was still too fat? She was sure she'd dropped several dress sizes, if they ever let her put on a dress. Gordon just liked to use her, savagely and without regard to her sexuality. Gina was relieved to learn he was gay, as she assumed that meant he would leave her virtue intact. She was wrong about that, of course.

• • •

One day while Gina was sitting up on the counter for their daily ritual, legs spread wide while Frank shaved her pussy to smooth silk, he said, "I wonder what you'd look like making yourself come." Gina colored and looked down, saying nothing. She rarely spoke these days, having given up any protest to be set free. She sometimes went whole days without even thinking of her family or Dwayne. They were like some past life that continued to recede in the face of constant physical stimulation and torture. Her world had shrunk dramatically to her room, and the bathroom, and the two men who used her constantly, with brute force or with surprising gentleness, depending on the man and the situation.

"It isn't a sin, you know," he remarked as he expertly smoothed baby oil onto her denuded flesh. She looked at him then, startled. That very thought had in fact just inserted itself into her brain, a persistent, nagging reminder of the life she used to adhere to so rigorously. It was no longer her first thought, this focus on sin and redemption that had so controlled her conscious thought before the abduction. Now it snuck in the back door, taking second or third place behind what Gordon was going to do today, or if Frank would visit her. Whether she would be beaten or "forced" to come, whether Frank would weigh her today, and reward her or punish her according to her progress.

But his direct statement forced her to focus and she listened as he went on. "Sin is an offense, a reprehensible act against God. Touching your body, how can that be sinful? Giving yourself pleasure, where is the crime? It seems to me that if God created your body as a temple, what better way to worship him than to treat that temple with love, to make it feel good?"

Gina didn't answer, but she ruminated over what he had said. Where was the harm? Why had her pastor railed so at them about the sins of the flesh? How did this compare to lying or stealing or worshipping false gods? Gina thought back to her confirmation, when the pastor had droned on about the body and spirit being diametrically opposed, and how the body was a repository of evil and filth, to be used only for procreation. She hadn't questioned it at the time, but she had been filled with shame, loathing even, about her then changing and maturing body. The soft hair sprouting under her arms and on her privates had disgusted her, and her budding breasts had embarrassed her. She realized now that that was when she had first turned to food for comfort. She felt safe, like the little girl she still longed to be. Her mother and later Dwayne had encouraged her in this, always plying her with goodies, and praising her for acting like a child.

Why had it never bothered her before? Her thoughts were interrupted by Frank's words, which jerked her back to the present. "I want to watch you make yourself come, Gina. I'm going to teach you the art of self-stimulation. It's time we made a woman of you, and a proper slave slut girl. Gordon has told me he wants to watch, but I convinced him you need lessons first. He has little patience for the novice, and I don't think you'd be able to come yet from having your cunt caned, which is what would end up happening, if I know Gordon, and I do.

Gina's eyes widened in horror. Frank went on, "No, I convinced him, and we'll begin our lessons today. You've already become such a cum-slut that it shouldn't be a problem." Frank grinned but Gina blushed anew. Yet even as he spoke, she felt her pussy tighten in anticipation. Always naked, stroked, aroused, beaten, humiliated, exposed, day after day, Gina's focus was, not surprisingly, on her body, on sensation, good or bad. Sometimes they blurred and she was confused, as a spanking became a massage, Frank's fingers trailing to her spread pussy, or a whipping softened to a caress.

Not so with Gordon. With him she knew exactly where she stood, or more accurately where she knelt. He used her brutally, and there was rarely any sexual content to their sessions, though he did abuse her breasts, pussy, and ass perhaps more than the rest of her always naked body. But his pleasure didn't depend on hers, as Frank's seemed to. It was almost as if Frank were her lover! Gina actually felt a twinge of pleasure at the thought, and at the same time a twinge of guilt, since she was betrothed to another, to Dwayne, though that life seemed like a dream now.

"Okay, you're done. Let's go to your room and start our lesson." Frank led her down the hall that connected her world. He instructed her to sit in a corner and then he blindfolded her and told her to sit still. Gina did so, curious as to why, but silent as usual. She heard Frank leave the room, and then return. She heard him moving about the space. Finally, he returned to her and took off the blindfold. Gina's eyes widened as she took in her transformed space. Instead of harsh light reflected off the mirrored walls, the room was illuminated with softly burning candles, a myriad of them, and the floor was covered with several silk spreads, and large soft pillows scattered about. The mirrors caught the soft light and threw it back again, so the room was literally aglow.

"It's lovely," she whispered, enchanted. Frank grinned, obviously pleased.

"Thought this would help with the mood. Come and lie down here." He pointed to a cluster of pillows and silk and Gina came obediently, lying down where he indicated. He kissed and licked the fingers of her right hand and then directed her fingers down to her pussy. She looked up at him, embarrassed, but also curious. She had never dared to play with herself before, even during the long idle hours when she was left alone in her prison.

But now she was being forced to; she had no choice. And so she began to touch herself, delicately at first, and then in imitation of the swirling massaging movements that Frank had used on her so many times. She felt pleasure begin to build and she stopped for a moment, confused and unsure.

"Don't stop," Frank urged her, and for emphasis he slapped her face, not too hard, and jerked her head back by the hair. She began to touch herself again, her face stinging, the pain from his pulling her hair and the slap to her cheek mixing with the sharp pleasure she was producing in her belly. Every time she slowed he slapped her and jerked her head back, and she'd rub herself harder, faster, until her eyes would flutter closed and she was lost in the sensation.

She was near to orgasm now, and having been well trained, she whispered, "May I?"

"Yes." And she did.

But the lesson wasn't over. "That was good," Frank said, his voice husky and low. "But once isn't enough for a slut like you. You have to do it again and again, for the pleasure of your master. So we start again."

Gina didn't want to start again. She wanted to lean back and revel in the endorphins coursing through her. She was delighted at having given herself such pleasure. She was amazed she had gone through her life never daring to do what she had just done so easily.

"I said again!" Frank punctuated his words with a slap to each cheek. Gina cried out and quickly moved her hand back to her now engorged and sensitive pussy lips. Frank leaned over and kissed her full on the mouth as she began to massage and tease her own clit. She was surprised to realize she was aroused again. She found she liked his kiss. His breath smelled sweet and she could also smell his cologne, something lemony and spicy.

He bit her lower lip gently, and then kissed her again. She kissed him back, hesitant at first, then with ardor. He didn't stop her. Her fingers forgot their dance as her arms encircled him. Frank pulled away suddenly, gruff. "Did I tell you to stop?" He looked disheveled, confused, almost afraid. Was the toy getting to him?

Reluctantly, Gina put her hand back to her pussy and closed her eyes, still feeling the imprint of his kiss on her mouth. She wanted to hate him, did hate him on an obvious level, for keeping her here, for letting Gordon hurt her, but a part of her now surfaced, still feeling the kiss, still wanting that kiss. Confused like he was, she shut down her mind and focused on her task.

Again her whispered request and then the spasms of orgasm. The third time was harder; she didn't want to do it and her labia were getting sore. Frank squeezed some KY jelly across her pussy and pressed her fingers into the goo. It did make things easier, and again Gina worked on arousing herself. This time when she asked for permission to come Frank said, "No."

Gina's eyes opened wide, and she tried to stop the tremors that had started in her. "I said no, Gina. No. Take your hand away." Gina did so, but it was too late, she was already caught in the throes of release, and he knew it. "Bad girl," he whispered, his eyes glinting in the flickering light. "Now you'll have to be punished." Another set up. She knew it, but what could she do? "I'm going to invite Gordon to this little show. He has told me he wants to see how I discipline you." In point of fact, Frank rarely disciplined Gina. She obeyed him and he didn't seem to favor whippings or spankings just for fun, as Gordon did.

Gina was scared now, and she hugged herself, rocking back and forth, biting her lower lip. Gordon and Frank had never been in the room with her at the same time. She thought of them as completely separate, as two very different parts of her day, of her life. She realized she didn't want to share Frank with Gordon. She didn't want to see Frank the slave boy, with Gordon the master. And yet, at the same time, she was suddenly intrigued at the notion. What would happen? What would the interplay be? Would the focus not be so entirely on her for a change? Would she get to see them interact as slave and master? But Gina had never seen a submissive who was trying to impress his master. She was unaware that a slave is sometimes more brutal than the master would ever be.

Frank instructed Gina to clean up the room, stacking everything neatly by the door. She did as she was ordered, sighing as she blew out the sweetly scented candles, and as she folded the soft sheets and moved the pillows. Frank had flicked the harsh fluorescent lights back on as he had left the room, the switch being located just outside of her door, and she was again in the sterile bright cage that she had barely left for the weeks she had been held captive.

Frank returned in a few minutes with a stool, which he placed in the center of the room under the pulley and hook contraption in the ceiling, and with several feet of chain, coiled neatly on a spool. He put a small pillow on the stool and told Gina to sit down.

Gina was passive as Frank attached her leather ankle and wrist straps, as well as a larger strap around her waist. Each strap was secured with a clip, and to these clips he attached lengths of chain. He didn't speak to her as he worked, but climbed a stepladder he had placed near her for the purpose, and secured the chains together to the pulley. When he did this, Gina lost her balance as he pulled and maneuvered the chains, forcing her back so that she was chained by her wrists, ankles and waist to the ceiling, with only her bare bottom balancing on the stool. The straps were lined with fleece, and he hadn't stretched her limbs so far that it hurt. Gina would be able to stay suspended like this for a long time, and indeed, that was the intention. Frank adjusted the pulley mechanism until her arms were stretched out above her head, and her legs were spread far apart, revealing the dark pink petals of her pussy and the little bud of her asshole.

Gina was actually grateful for the blindfold he slipped over her eyes. She couldn't tolerate the embarrassment she still felt at seeing her naked and splayed body mirrored back to her from all angles. While she had grown used to being naked at all times, she still could not look at her own private parts without flushing with shame. The fact that she was completely shaved made it that much more humiliating for her. The silken blindfold at least spared her from having to look, though she knew her captors could look all they like, and she could not close her legs, completely immobilized as she was.

"Frank, I'm scared." This outburst was not typical, for Gina now rarely spoke. But that kiss, it had somehow emboldened her. When he had pulled away, she had seen, just for that moment, his vulnerability, his desire for her. And so she dared to take this liberty and speak without being spoken to.

"You should be," was all he said, and Gina began to tremble. She believed him completely.

Satisfied at last with his arrangements, Frank left the room. He returned with Gordon, and as they entered, Gina heard Gordon say, "So she came without permission, huh? Do you remember what I did to you when that happened, Frank?" Gina didn't hear any response, but she heard Gordon's abrupt laugh as he said, "Ah! I see you do remember! Do you think this cunt can withstand what you did? She is, after all, only a *woman*." The word woman was spat out, like an epithet.

"I guess we'll see what she can take, sir," Frank said quietly, his voice subdued and respectful.

"Well, see that you whip her properly. If I think your effort is half-hearted, I'll take the job over myself." Though Gina couldn't see him, Frank's face burned with Gordon's implication that he wasn't up to the job, but he only bowed his head, saying nothing. Then Gina heard that whistling sound she had never forgotten since that first week when Gordon had caned her. Involuntarily, she gave a little cry of fear. Instinctively she tried to close her legs, but the chains held her firmly in place, completely exposed.

She cried out again, startled as she felt fingers on her thighs. They were Frank's hands, large and cool against her flesh. As he caressed her, she relaxed slightly, but adrenaline coursed through her body, making her giddy and constricting her breathing. She felt his warm breath as he leaned near her ear and whispered, "Courage, dear heart."

Then, without warning, he struck her inner thigh with the cane. A line of pain seared her, but before she could focus on it, there was another whistle and another cut, this time to the other thigh. Gina screamed, and then her howl was cut off as a smaller hand, but still a very strong one, clamped over her mouth. Gina felt panicked, since the hand partially covered her nose as well and she couldn't breathe. She struggled and cried out under the hand, and mercifully, Gordon moved enough so that she could breathe, but he kept his hand firmly over her mouth.

"Take it, cunt," he hissed. "And next time show some discipline over your orgasms, you whore." Again the cane, slicing her flesh from side to side until her legs felt flayed, as if they were being burned and cut all at once. It took her a moment or two to realize when it had stopped. The stinging of a thousand bees washed over her inner thighs, but Gordon had removed his hand and she gulped in the air between sobs.

The cane was brought to her face. Between shuddering breaths she managed to kiss the offending object. "Nice," Gordon murmured, as he examined her thighs, tender and welted, a crisscross of red lines on soft white flesh. "Tell me, Frank, is the whore wet? Did she get off on it like you do?" Frank leaned forward and touched her entrance with a finger. He slid the finger up, gently, to her clit, and swirled a teasing circle for a few moments. Gina's sobbing had subsided, and now just the sound of her rapid breathing filled the air.

As he brought his finger lower, he found to his surprise that she was wet! Was it only his hand just now that had aroused her? Was she so conditioned now by his touch that she got wet? Or could the beating have somehow transmuted into some kind of pleasure for her? He well understood the feeling; he was trained himself just this way. For Gina, these past several weeks of constant stimulation, of pain purposefully mixed with pleasure, was designed precisely to cue her body from either angle. A whipping or a kiss was to have the same effect, that of arousal, of desire, of submission and an implicit need to obey. And here she was, his little slave girl, wet from a caning that had left her marked and bruised. Frank's reverie was disturbed by Gordon who said, "Well?"

"She is. The slut is wet." Frank grinned at Gordon, who instantly grasped the implication of the success of their training to date. Not that he had doubted it. He had trained dozens of slaves, and though there were some who never took to it, most did, eventually. Perhaps there is something in each of us that longs to submit, if the seed of it is properly nurtured.

Gordon laughed, a low, cruel sound, and then said, "Let's leave her here for a while. Let her think on her 'sins.'" He laughed again and gestured toward the door. Frank went first, followed by Gordon, who ripped the blindfold from Gina's face as he passed.

Left alone, Gina lay still for a long time, not even opening her eyes against the bright light. The pain on her thighs had subsided to a dull, itchy sting, and she longed to touch herself there, to sooth the tattered flesh. Her limbs had begun to ache, and her bottom was asleep. She thought about what they had said. She did feel a faint throb in her clit and deep in her pussy. What was becoming of her? A whipping made her wet? She was no better than the fallen girls in the bad part of town she used to smugly look down on while she tried to counsel them about the ways of the Lord.

But perhaps no worse? It was a novel thought, and one Frank had been trying to teach her; there is nothing inherently wrong with sex, or your body, or desire. The overlay of torture and captivity made it confusing, but she was beginning to grasp, even to believe, the underlying message of sex and sexuality as neutral or even good things, not simply tools for procreation.

As she thought about this some more, she tried to lift her head, to see herself suspended and spread on the stool. There in front of her was a long legged woman, not quite trim, but certainly no longer plump, with her long dark hair streaming down behind her. Gina barely recognized the strong new body that was emerging from the formerly dumpy shape she was used to seeing, or more accurately, avoiding, in the mirror.

Then she focused on her bare and spread pussy, on the labia that looked curiously like rose petals. Why had she found it so repulsive before? It was almost beautiful! It looked like a pink flower, dark against the white flesh of her thighs, matching the color of the red welts the cane had raised. She stared for a while at the crisscross of welts. She had endured a caning and felt a peculiar sense of pride.

But she was thirsty, and her limbs ached. She wished Frank would come and release her. Finally, she heard the knob turn, the key scrap, and she became alert at once, rousing herself from the half sleep into which she had fallen. Both men entered again, and Gina felt a keen dismay that Gordon was there too. They were both in bathrobes, and it looked as if they wore nothing underneath. Frank approached Gina and said, "We've decided it's time for you to become a woman, in the full sense of the word."

Gina looked at him, a question in her eyes. Gordon elaborated. "What my boy is trying to say in his poetic way is that it's time you learned how to be fucked. The virgin has become a slut and now it's time you were shown what a cock feels like in that tight little twat of yours. You are going to be fucked."

Gina's mouth had opened into a silent O, but no words were formed. She had been wondering when this would happen; knew it was only a matter of time and had been frankly surprised, though also relieved, that it hadn't happened sooner. But she had never thought Gordon would be witness. She had assumed, because he was gay, that he wouldn't want anything to do with it. Of course, now she realized he might want to watch, to control the proceedings since he owned both of them, in his mind.

She didn't want him there, of course, but what choice did she have? At least they would take her down? Let her be comfortable? Frank came over to her, cradled her head in his hands and whispered, "Don't worry, I'll be right here. Just relax and it will be fine." He stayed by her head, and to Gina's horror, it was Gordon who disrobed, positioning himself between her legs.

She stared in helpless fascination at his naked body, at his large semi-erect cock. Her heart had begun to pound and she felt panic rising in her throat like bile. Frank sensed her distress, and she felt his hand on her cheek, soothing her, silently willing her to calm down.

"Make me hard, boy," Gordon commanded, and Frank quickly left Gina to kneel in front of his master. With skill and speed, he took Gordon's cock deep into his throat, moaning slightly as Gordon pulled against the back of his head, and then slowly began to thrust in and out of Frank's mouth. Gina was horrified, but at the same time fascinated by what she was witnessing. She watched with what she wouldn't have admitted was almost admiration for the way Frank could remain per-fectly still, Gordon's cock thrust deep in his throat. He didn't pull back or resist in the slightest while Gordon used his mouth. After just a few minutes Gordon pushed Frank away, and Frank came back to her, wiping his face on his sleeve.

Gordon's penis was erect now, glistening with Frank's saliva. He moved toward the suspended woman's spread and gaping pussy. Using his hand to guide it in, Gordon pushed his penis against her opening, pressing until it popped in, ignoring her cries of fear and pain. "It's almost as tight as your lovely ass," he remarked, grinning at Frank as he began to rape the young woman bound in chains. "Stop her noise, she's distracting me."

Gina might have expected a hand to be clamped over mouth and nose, but instead Frank muffled her cries with his own kiss, smoothing back her hair and holding her gently. Gordon was careful at first, but insistent. He pressed his large impossibly hard cock against Gina's small opening, holding her legs apart with strong hands on either thigh. Her legs were still hot from the savage whipping she had endured, and he knew his hands must have felt like sandpaper against her injured flesh.

He marveled silently at his own arousal, even though this was just a woman, but he understood himself and what he was doing well enough to know this wasn't about sex, but about power. Yes, he would choose a male lover, but when it came to the toys, when it came to using them, to breaking them, to torturing them, he didn't care about their sex. He cared about their ability to suffer, their sensitivity, and their terror. And Gina had all these lovely qualities in spades. She was turning out to be their most responsive slave to date and now she was being given the ultimate test.

Frank stood at Gina's head, holding her arms, which were still chained and extended to the ceiling. The stool on which Gina's bare ass rested was just the right height for Gordon as he leaned over to fuck her. The crisscross of welts on her thighs, the tangle of dark hair over white breasts, his slave boy standing over her, it was such an arousing image that Gordon could no longer contain himself. He plunged into the chained virgin; he raped her. Her cunt was deliciously tight, and sheer physical pleasure pulsed into power as he brutally fucked her.

Gordon pulled out just before coming, and spurted his semen over her belly, and on the welted, creamy thighs of his victim. He wouldn't waste his seed in some cunt. Gina's face was obscured by Frank's head, her whimpers muffled, as he still leaned over her, protectively Gordon thought, feeling a hint of annoyance. He pushed down any misgivings and, pulling on his robe, said only, "Clean her up." There was a faint trickle of blood where he had torn the virgin flesh. "Let's leave her up for a while. I need a shower." Frank followed his master, his expression inscrutable.

Chapter 5

THE PUPPY DOG

It seemed Frank had only been waiting for Gordon's first use. The master had defiled the slave girl, and now she was *available* for use. That was how Gina figured it, and in fact she was quite right. Gordon's claiming of her virginity certainly had little to do with sex, and nothing to do with love. It was a rape, pure and simple. An assertion of his power. He did it, in a word, because he could.

Frank came to her the next morning, and after the daily cleansing ritual, he had led her back to her mirrored room and told her, "Today I'm going to make love to you." He didn't mention that he had been waiting for this moment. His master didn't like girls, but whenever they had one, he was always the first to use her pussy, to claim her in that way. Once he had done it, he lost interest. They had kidnapped several women over the years, as well as several men. The women were much easier to control, of course. The men tended to fight more; to be more physical. But in the end, they all capitulated, all became willing slaves, living, it seemed, only to please their masters.

But this was the first time Frank had felt something akin to bitterness as he watched Gordon rape Gina. Still, he had to admit that he had liked kissing her mouth while she trembled and shuddered beneath him. The idea of holding down the virgin for such a primal offering certainly had its appeal. But something was different here.

Usually he was at worst indifferent, at best excited as he watched his master. He didn't understand this new feeling, though on further reflection he had to admit it must be jealousy! He certainly wasn't jealous regarding Gordon. Though Gordon used Frank roughly, Frank felt secure in his position as head slave. So it must be Gina who had made him jealous! He realized with a sense of confusion that he had wanted to be the first one to fuck her. He hadn't dared voice this to Gordon, who would have taken offense if Frank seemed to be regarding one of their toys as anything more than an object for their amusement.

Yes, something was different here. Something about her eyes; something about the way she stared at him, so silent now, but as if she were speaking directly to his heart. It unnerved him, because it was a new experience. He found that he thought of her as a person, and that he didn't like it sometimes when Gordon was especially brutal. He found he wanted to protect her.

Frank didn't know what to do with these new feelings, and for the most part, he was able to ignore them. Gordon had always given him free rein with the toys while he was at work, and when he was home, Frank made sure Gordon was satisfied and cared for. But while Gordon was gone, Frank was in total control.

Gina had been asleep when he opened the door, though she startled awake, as she always did, when he came in. He saw her relax, understanding that she wanted to see him, not because he was Frank, but because he was not Gordon. He said, more gruffly than he intended, "Lie down and spread your legs; I want to inspect any damage." Gina obeyed him, jumping slightly as his finger touched the still tender area of her entrance. Gordon had torn the skin slightly, but it was already almost healed, after just a night of rest. Her thighs were still mottled and bruised from the caning.

Gina didn't want to be fucked. She still remembered Gordon's hard penis pressing mercilessly into her, and she covered her pussy with her hands, as if that would protect her from Frank. She loved the new sensation of orgasm, but Gordon's rape had nothing to do with pleasure. She clamped her hands down tighter over her bare sex.

Frank gently pulled her hands away and she didn't dare resist. His heart melted at the fear in her face. "Shh, don't worry, sweetheart. I'm not Gordon. I won't hurt you. This can be a lovely experience, you know. It doesn't have to hurt."

Gina didn't believe him, but she was not in a position to argue. Carefully, Frank lay next to Gina. She could feel his penis as it pressed hard through the denim of his jeans against her bare thigh. Frank kissed

Gina's face, nuzzling her neck and moving lower with his mouth down her belly.

The sweet spicy smell of her made him hungry to taste her, and his mouth sought out her pussy. Holding her wrists tightly on either side of her body, Frank kissed and teased Gina until she was moaning with pleasure. He rarely kissed her in this way, but when he did, he loved the way she shivered and moaned, arching against him as she became aroused.

Before it went too far, he stopped and stood up, unzipping his jeans, revealing an erect cock, no underwear. Gina looked at him with fear in her face, but he dropped quickly down onto her, determined to fuck her now. Her entrance was still slick and wet from his kisses, and he pressed just the head of his cock into her, allowing her time to get used to the invading presence. Gina was still aroused from his kisses and her own near orgasm. She had become sensitized to his constant stimulation over the time she had been their prisoner, and she was used to being allowed sexual release.

He teased her, staying very still, and then moving slightly into her. Gina arched up slightly, seeming to want more. He smiled to himself and pulled away, causing her to move in toward him. The wench wanted it! He continued to tease her, pressing in just the head, and then withdrawing, until she actually moaned in frustration. He could feel that she was wet and needy. All at once, he thrust his rigid cock into her pussy, and Gina grunted involuntarily.

Frank lay still for a moment, his weight pinning her down, his hands on her wrists, which he now held over her head. As he bent down to kiss her neck, Frank began to move slowly in and out, careful not to hurt her. Gina was fully primed, her eyes closed, lips apart, skin flushed.

Frank's dominant side asserted itself as his passion took over, and he began to fuck her hard and fast, using her for his pleasure. His balls were tight with need as they slapped against her ass. She was responding, not with fear or pain, as she had with Gordon, but with the mature and needy pleasure of a woman in lust. He pulled out suddenly and commanded, "Turn over."

Gina didn't understand at first, until he flipped her and half-pulled, half-pushed her to her hands and knees so he could take her from behind. They could see themselves in the mirrors, the tall, strong man, his large hands holding her hips, and the pale women on her knees, dark hair curling over her shoulders, obscuring her face.

She saw his large cock slide in between her ample ass cheeks, seeking out her tight but very wet cunt. She felt the pleasure course up through her belly as he entered her again. As he fucked her, his head fell back, eyes closed. He was using her, hard, and she realized that the sight of them in the mirrors aroused and fascinated her almost as much as the physical action of his lovemaking.

Suddenly, an unwelcome vision of her fiancé, the reliable and plodding Dwayne, came into her mind's eye. He was looking at her disapprovingly, and she knew he would be stunned and confused by what was happening. His large pink face dissolved into the stern features of her father, who she knew without a doubt would condemn her out of hand. He could never understand or forgive her for what had happened, even though it was so obviously beyond her control. Victim and perpetrator had always been painted with the same brush in his book, both doomed to hell, without the possibility of redemption. Gina remembered how he had reacted when she tried to talk about a rape victim at a shelter whom she had tried to counsel. Her father had silenced her, intoning about Jezebel, and whores deserving what they get.

Gina's pensive thoughts were obliterated at that moment when Frank reached under her and began to massage her clit while he continued to pummel her pussy. Giving in to the pure pleasure, Gina felt the lovely rolling sensation of approaching orgasm. Her breathless request for release was met with a loud and extended, "Yes!" as Frank came hard inside of her. They fell together to the floor, rolling in a lovers' embrace, his cock still deep inside of her. Yes, they were almost like lovers, except that lovers have a choice, and Gina had none.

• • •

One morning when Gina awoke, she heard rain falling, pummeling the roof, pattering against windows somewhere else in the house. While she was still expected to train and to practice the art of becoming a submissive slut, Frank now fucked her at least once a day, and it had nothing to do with training. There was no denying that the pleasure was now mutual. She had given herself to him completely, and she lived for the moments when he came to her, for what else was there?

As the rain continued its lilting song, Gina thought about being outside, smelling fresh air, seeing her mother. She thought about sunlight, and the pattern of shadows it left. There were no shadows in this fluorescent-lit room. Would she ever leave this room? If she were set free, could she return to her home? Could she assume the mantel of "good little girl" again? Was she only behaving this way now to avoid being punished or worse? Or had something actually changed inside of her, something she could never pretend away or undo just by wishing? What was the point of wondering? This was her reality now.

She lay quietly on her mattress, tapping a song with the silver spoon Frank had left for her to practice with. The mattress was thin and she could feel the hard floor beneath it, but she was used to it. She stared up at the ceiling, examining the pulley apparatus that had held her, suspended and helpless, so many times now she had lost count. She thought about the two men who had become her world. Gordon, with his boyish good looks, his cold gray eyes and his cruel tongue, and Frank, tall and lanky, almost adolescent sometimes in his awkwardness. She smiled slightly, thinking about the way he seemed to take such pleasure in preparing low-calorie foods for her, in watching her transform from chubby girl to lithe woman, in using her body for his pleasure. And hers.

She had never expected to love being fucked. She even liked the word now. It was earthy and without pretense or euphemism. Certainly the first time with Gordon had been horrible, a terrifying and painful ordeal. And even before that, before she had become their prisoner, her mother had vaguely but darkly hinted that sex was something to be tolerated; it was a duty, certainly not a pleasure. The idea of oral sex was completely beyond her mother's ken, of that Gina was certain. And the concept of sex for pleasure, especially for the woman's pleasure, was also alien to her.

But not to Gina. In fact, sex was one of her sole pleasures now, and she spent a lot of time thinking about it. Even now her idle hands began to move down her body, to feel the new muscles in her arms and calves. She felt the unfamiliar tautness of her stomach muscles, and the long smooth muscles in her thighs. She actually liked her body now. She even liked the total smoothness that was the result of the daily shaving. She looked forward to her mornings in the bathroom with Frank, her excursion outside of the mirrored room.

The rain was a steady peaceful patter, and, spoon forgotten, her fingers began an unconscious rhythm of their own on her belly. They slipped down to her bare pussy. She liked the feel of the plump outer lips and the soft tender inner lips. Moving slightly, she spread her legs and brought fingers wet with her own kiss to her pussy.

Gina felt a momentary pang of guilt; even of fear. This wasn't her body, as Gordon told her over and over. It was his. That's what he said, but she secretly regarded it more as Frank's. Frank, the admitted slave boy and lover of Gordon, was still her "master" in the sense that he controlled her every move when he was with her, and decided her daily routine, even down to when or if she could pee or have a drink of water. And he was the one who made her come, over and over again.

Her fingers gently parted the smooth shaven cleft of her pussy, and she slid one finger up into the velvet softness of her vagina. With her other hand, she began to rub and tease her clit, arching up slightly to get a better angle. She saw the young woman in the mirror, naked, hands between her legs. This time she didn't turn away in shame, but stared at her new slender image, startled at how beautiful she looked. Then in her mind's eye she saw Frank, her first and only lover. She almost felt his kiss as her fingers moved faster and her pleasure mounted. She almost heard his voice, whispering her name over and over.

Frank came into the room suddenly, startling Gina, confusing her as the dream Frank was suddenly standing in front of her, very real. She quickly slammed her legs closed, all thought of a stolen orgasm obliterated. "Obedience," Frank announced cryptically, seemingly unaware that his toy had been using the master's body without permission. As Gina knelt before him, as she had been taught, Frank said, "Today we will work on your obedience. The master wants to fuck your ass. Oh, save the startled bird look. Surely you've known it was coming. He likes boys, don't forget, and that is one thing you have in common with us boys." Frank grinned. Gordon wanted that last bastion of virginity violated. Frank said her first task was to desensitize herself about her asshole. God, she couldn't even think the word itself without blushing slightly. Asshole.

Always in tune with her, Frank sensed this shyness and made her say the word over and over. "Asshole," she had whispered. Louder. "Asshole. Asshole! Asshole!" She ended up yelling it, and suddenly they both laughed. It was the first time she had laughed, certainly since she had been taken hostage however many weeks ago. She didn't know how long she'd been here. Time was marked by eating, exercise, sleeping, showers, grooming, torture sessions, play sessions, and daydreams. There was no day; no night. The past was receding like a long forgotten dream. The future didn't exist; there was only now.

When he ordered her to kneel and spread her ass cheeks to show him her asshole and to look at it in the mirror, she felt heat flame through her face and creep down her chest. But somehow she complied, her eyes squeezed shut so she wouldn't have to see herself in the mirror, lewdly displayed from all angles.

Then Frank gave her an order she couldn't obey. She wouldn't. He dropped his pants and said, "You may as well get used to this now, because it's going to happen some time. Gordon likes homage paid to his asshole by us lowly slave types. That includes you. I'm a nice guy, and I know you're a shy girl, so I'm going to let you practice on me. Don't worry, I showered this morning." Frank knelt, revealing his bare ass, whose cheeks he spread so that Gina had a clear view of his asshole. He didn't seem in the slightest bit embarrassed. He had been in this position many times, with many more observers than just a little toy slut.

"Okay, baby. All you have to do is lick it a little. I won't make you do a reaming, not yet. Time to get used to it. Just kneel there and lick my asshole. It's a humbling experience, no question. A real submissive rush. Just accept it as part of your homage to your master. I know you can do it."

Gina crouched behind the tall man whose ass was exposed to her. Even as her brain ordered her to comply to avoid punishment, something in her couldn't seem to obey. Even though Frank hadn't specifically told her she'd be punished if she failed to obey, it was understood. Though he treated her with love and even respect, when she failed in a task he had set for her, he always punished her, and sometimes severely. He had learned well from his master and he wasn't at all squeamish about inflicting pain. In fact, he enjoyed it; Frank was perhaps one of the few true "switches" in the world of doms and subs.

But Gina realized she'd rather be punished than do what he was asking. She had been subjected to many bizarre tortures, but being asked to tongue someone's asshole seemed an impossible task. Perhaps the difference was that she was given so few tasks which she had to perform on her own. More often she was subjected to various tortures and pleasures. Rarely was she asked to actively perform, with the exception of cocksucking, at which she was now adept.

Frank waited patiently for a few moments, saying nothing, waiting to feel her wet little tongue against his ass. When nothing happened, he stood up, looking sternly at the still kneeling Gina who was hiding her face in her hands. He didn't beat her, or force her. Instead, he said in a quiet voice, "When you're ready to obey, let me know. Then you can have your breakfast." As soon as he mentioned breakfast, she realized she was hungry, but he was out the door, and the lock clicked into place. Minutes slipped into an hour, two hours, and finally he returned.

She knelt before him, ready to try, and again her tongue defied her.

Frank didn't cajole or threaten, he just left. The third time it must have been late afternoon, and when she still didn't obey, she was left thirsty, ravenous, and alone. That was probably her longest night, longer even than the day Gordon had raped her, and they had left her hanging for several hours, whipped legs spread wide. Then, at least her mind had been a turmoil of emotion, and that and her spent body had allowed her to drop from exhaustion when she was finally let down. But now there was just her empty belly, her dry throat, and the knowledge that she still had a test to pass—one she had failed already three times.

The next morning found Gina in a fitful sleep when Gordon came in, followed by Frank. Both men looked grim as Gina scrambled up to kneel before them, head low and arms outstretched as Gordon liked. "Good morning, cunt," said the master.

"Good morning . . ." Gina coughed and tried to clear her throat, which was scratchy and parched with thirst. Hunger had shrunk to a little gnawing in her belly, but it was the thirst that consumed her thoughts. She began again. "Good morning, sir. I am your slave cunt."

"Prove it. Stop this crap and do what you're told. If you think one day without food and water is hard, try three." As he spoke, Frank kneeled quietly, baring his own ass for Gina's tentative tongue. Her thirst and fear of Gordon overcame any last trepidation she had. Closing her eyes, Gina snaked out her tongue and gingerly touched Frank's little puckered asshole. Gordon came up behind and pushed her head so that her face was mashed against Frank's ass. Holding her there he said, "See, that isn't so bad, now is it? Now we're going to speed up this anal training business. I'm getting tired of your bullshit. You will obey to the letter. Got it, cunt? Now, kneel down and show me your asshole, back toward the mirror. Spread 'em. Now." He thrust her forward toward a mirror.

This time she obeyed at once, kneeling on the hard floor, head touching it, ass in the air. Her face flamed, but she managed to hold the position while both men knelt, carefully inspecting her virgin bottom. Gordon grabbed her by the hair and jerked her head, forcing her to look at her image in the glass. She looked down, but her eyes didn't focus; he couldn't make her focus on her asshole, and she felt secretly proud of this tiny act of defiance.

When he let her go, Gina whispered, "Please, sir?"

"Please what?" Gordon smiled, but the curl of his mouth was cruel.

"Water?"

"After we plug your nasty little asshole, then you can have a drink from a bowl like the bad little puppy you are." Gina cried out in dismay, trying to scoot away from the two men, but of course it was useless.

Frank held her down while Gordon greased and inserted a small anal plug into her ass. It happened quite fast. Gina yelped, but she didn't struggle. There was a moment of pain as the plug pressed past her sphincter, and then a snugness, but no real discomfort. As with so many things, the fear of anticipation was worse than the actual deed.

She stared at the floor, humiliated and ashamed, as Frank filled a metal bowl with cool water. "Go on, doggy," taunted Gordon. "Have a bit of water and then you can do some tricks for us." Gina crawled over to the water bowl, desperate for a drink. Awkwardly she licked the water, splashing it on the floor and herself in her efforts to get enough.

While she was drinking, Gordon slipped a collar around her neck, secured by Velcro and a clip he slipped onto a ring at the back of it. He clipped a leash onto the collar and, before she could get her fill, he jerked her roughly away from the bowl. Water spilled down her chin and between her breasts. She was still thirsty, but the most desperate need had been slaked.

"Would you like to go for walk, doggie?" Gordon pulled her roughly, leading her around the room as she tried to keep up without stumbling. "Should we take the dog out to pee, Frank? Let her sniff in the back yard?" Outside? Was he serious, would they really let her go outside? Even on a leash, dragged by her neck, Gina was longing to go outside, to smell the fresh air, to feel the sun!

"I don't know, sir," Frank answered. "It is drizzling, after all. And still pretty cold."

"So we'll wear raincoats. And bitches don't need coats, they're animals. Let's do it!" Frank didn't look too happy, but he didn't protest. Opening the door, he allowed Gordon to pass through, pulling the poor naked woman behind him on her leash.

They led her the other way down the hall, away from Gina's bathroom. They passed into a large room with soft throw rugs scattered over hardwood floors. Gina didn't have adequate time to take in the details, but she could see a fire crackling in the fireplace. The room was decorated in warm yellows and browns. The sofas looked plump and inviting.

Gordon continued to pull Gina until they were at the back door, which was set in a small foyer containing an antique wardrobe. Frank opened the wardrobe doors and took out an umbrella and two gray trench coats. He held one coat open, and Gordon slipped his arms in and buttoned himself up. Frank did the same, leaving the hapless Gina naked and collared at their feet.

When Gordon opened the back door, Gina felt a gust of cold wet air against her bare flanks. She shivered as he pulled her out into the back yard, which was completely enclosed by tall dense hedges of evergreen. Though the clouds hid the sun, the natural light was beautiful to Gina. The rain pelted her bare back and legs, and the grass was slick and cold under her hands and knees. She felt the cold slice through her like a knife, and was afraid of what Gordon had planned for her, but she couldn't help but smile with pleasure at the heady smell of fresh rain and pine trees. She inhaled deeply the wet scented air.

Gordon jerked her chain and ordered, "Pee for us, dog. Right here in the grass." Gina looked miserably over at Frank, who turned away. Gordon jerked her chain again, causing Gina to fall sideways, landing on her side in the wet, muddy grass. She scrambled up, truly cold now and splattered with mud. "Do it and then you can come in."

Gina was shivering now, shuddering with cold and fear. She was dizzy with hunger. She squatted, trying to pee, hoping he meant what he said about that being all she had to do. But she couldn't. A few mouthfuls of water, after nothing to eat and drink the whole prior day, had left her dehydrated. She had nothing to void, no matter how badly she wanted to.

"Come on!" Gordon emphasized the last word with a strong smack to her wet ass. He continued to jerk the leash, while hitting her bare bottom, until Gina began to whimper and beg. She tried to squat, but he kept pulling her out of position, and then hitting her for failing to obey.

"She can't, sir," Frank said, finally stepping forward. "She hasn't had any food or water for 24 hours. She's got nothing to piss."

Gordon slapped her wet cheek. Unzipping his jeans, he pulled out his cock and forced it into Gina's mouth. He held her head, pressing his cock back into her throat, choking her with it. "Suck it, cunt. Show me how all those lessons on Frank have made you a cocksucking queen." Holding her head in both hands, he rammed his cock deep into her throat, giving Gina no chance to catch her breath. He was rough, but he was fast, and after just a few minutes he let her go, sending her sprawling back on the wet grass.

His semen mixed with the rain pelting on her bare belly. He was zipping up as Frank said, trying to keep his voice light, "Let's go in, Gordon. We don't want a sick toy on our hands. Think how boring that would be." Gordon seemed to consider this, staring at the naked muddied girl gasping on the ground in front of him. Frank gently took the leash from Gordon, who made no protest, and led Gina, still on her hands and knees, back into the house.

Unlike Gordon, who had half dragged Gina on her leash, Frank went slowly, allowing her to keep her balance. He stopped in front of the fire, where Gina gratefully edged next to the hot flames, sniffling. She was a mess, hair wet and matted over her face, body wet and flecked with mud. The anal plug was still buried in her ass, but she didn't even notice it now, her sole preoccupation fixed on getting closer to that fire. Frank was using a large towel, wiping off some of the water, cum, and mud that covered Gina's naked body.

Gordon stood apart from the pair, his eyes hooded, expression closed. Pursing his lips he said, "All right Frank. You always were the one with common sense, I suppose. Though I'd like to have let her try a little longer. Go ahead, clean her off and get her back in her room. I think I'll go out. I'm finding the two of you a little tedious today." Frank watched him leave, and a worried look washed across his face.

But once Gordon had left the room, Frank helped Gina to her feet and as they walked back to her prison, he draped his arm protectively around her. First stop was the bathroom, where Frank poured a hot bath for the slave girl, adding the sweet smelling oils he had used that first time.

"Bend over," he ordered, and Gina blushed while he removed the little dildo from her ass and threw it into the sink. Then Frank helped his charge into the tub, leaving her to soak while he went to get her something to eat. He came back with a corn muffin, toasted with butter melting on top, and a steaming mug of coffee. Setting it next to the bath, he fed Gina little bits of the muffin as she soaked.

Slowly her body warmed, and she relaxed into the hot fragrant water. The corn muffin was the best thing she had ever tasted, and the coffee was hot and sweet, like caramel and cream. After weeks of broth and vegetables, it was quite a treat. Gina realized with surprise that she felt happy. The feeling was so alien, so new, like a fledgling little bird, mouth open, hungry for more. She smiled at Frank, who smiled back.

He had rarely seen that smile, being used to the pensive girl in repose, or the terrified slave being tortured, or the lust-filled woman racked in orgasm. But that smile! A pretty face was transformed into something radiant, like a private little dawn, and Frank felt his heart melt. He almost said aloud the words that had been slowly forming in his heart for some time now. Almost said them, but didn't, for the feelings confused and upset him.

She was his toy; his plaything. He and Gordon used their toys, and abused them, certainly they never loved them! There! He'd said it. Now he'd deny it. Perhaps to deceive himself, certainly to deceive her, Frank pushed down his newly admitted feelings. He realized that Gordon must have sensed this change in him as well. It would explain the man's abrupt departure, and his derisive comments about his two slaves before he left. Frank knew he would have to be very careful around Gordon for a while. He also knew he was in for a whipping himself this evening, and probably without the sexual overlay that usually defined his interaction with his master.

With these thoughts in his mind, Frank left Gina a towel and said tersely, "Dry yourself. Then go to your room. I'll bring you your meal and then I've got some work to do." Gina did as she was commanded, confused by his sudden withdrawal of affection. They had almost been friends for a moment. She had seen how he had stepped in for her; protected her from Gordon's craziness outside. She had also seen that Gordon seemed to be angry, and how he had left so abruptly.

She thought about the two of them, their complex relationship as lovers and as master and slave. It hadn't really occurred to her before now that Gordon might be in love with Frank, and vice versa. She didn't like the thought, felt possessive of Frank. Thinking of two men together still made her queasy, and she tried not to visualize what they must do when making love.

And now Gordon was hurt, perhaps jealous of what he sensed between Gina and Frank. And Frank, used to bending his own will entirely to Gordon's, had stood up to him, had taken the leash and literally as well as symbolically taken over control of Gina. But now Frank was gone, and Gina was alone in her room.

He brought in dinner, just a salad and seltzer, and left her without a word. She should have been delighted to be alone, to have escaped Gordon's wrath, but all she could think of was Frank's expression when Gordon had left them. No matter what she might fantasize went on between herself and Frank, clearly his heart, or at least his allegiance, was still with the master. Gina ate, barely tasting the food, and fell into an unsatisfactory and fitful doze.

The light was still on when Gina awoke and she had no idea what time it was, but something told her it was night. A sound outside her door must have awoken her. She heard the familiar sound of lock tumblers falling as the key turned and the door swung open, revealing Gordon, no shirt, blue jeans unbuttoned, hair tussled and falling over his eyebrow.

"Get up, cunt. I'm tired of watching Frank coddle you and treat you with kid gloves. Fuck that. I want to take your ass, and I am going to do just that. And, no, your knight in shining armor won't be coming to save you. He's, uh, tied up at the moment." He laughed at his own inside joke, as Frank was indeed tied up, wrists and ankles shackled to the bed where Gordon had just brutally sodomized him with a large rubber penis, leaving the offending article sticking out of his ass while he went to find Gina.

Gordon had been drinking, something he rarely did because he was aware of his own penchant for getting drunk. And he was, he knew, an ugly drunk. Sadism moved from carefully controlled and considered action to a restlessness and a cruelty which could be dangerous if unchecked. Gordon, sober, was a careful, even meticulous man who was always aware of his slaves' limits, even if he chose to violate them. But Gordon, drunk, was a man without scruples.

"Get up, cunt; it's your turn. I saved this all for you, baby. All for you." Gina stood uncertainly, fear breaking like a cold sweat over her body. She smelled the alcohol on his breath as Gordon roughly grabbed her hair, pulling her head back, holding her still as he kissed her. It wasn't like the slow sensual kisses Frank gave her. Gordon's kiss was an attack, a rape of her mouth. He thrust his tongue, forcing her teeth apart; an act of aggression.

"Come on, cunt. I'm going to show Frank how it's done." He grabbed Gina's wrist, pulling her into the hallway and through the living room to the bedroom where Frank was still tied down. Gina shrieked in horror when she saw Frank, the phallus rammed into his ass, face down in the pillow. Frank shifted, trying to lift his head when he heard them come in.

"Stay there!" Gordon ordered as he pushed Gina into a corner. Going over to Frank, Gordon removed a long thin sheath from his hip pocket, and Gina saw that it was a switchblade. The edge looked sharp and dangerous, as Gordon brought it close to Frank's face. Frank closed his eyes, making no protest. Gordon moved the blade and used it to cut the chords from Frank's wrists and ankles. He pulled the rubber dildo from Frank's ass and tossed it on the floor. As Frank massaged his wrists, Gordon said, "Stay there, boy. Position yourself so you can see. It's time you learned how to properly fuck a slave girl. How to rape a slave girl."

He laughed, his face more a grimace than a smile, and Gina shrunk back further into the corner. Gordon grabbed her wrist again and this time Gina actually pulled back, trying to get away. Gordon's face darkened, and he pulled out the knife, causing the blade to leap out with the flick of a button.

"How dare you, slut," he hissed, bringing the knife to her breast. "Have you learned nothing since you've been here? You don't resist me. Ever. I own you. I could kill you and no one would ever know. Got that, you bitch? You have no say. None. And neither does Frankie here. Now get down on the floor. Get your ass ready with this and consider yourself very lucky that I'm bothering with the lubricant. It's really for my comfort, not yours. I like an easy entrance." He tossed a tube of lubricating jelly toward the kneeling woman.

She opened the tube, fear making her movements jerky. She felt stunned by the naked Frank and how he had been bound. She had known intellectually that Frank was Gordon's slave boy, but she had never had it so clearly demonstrated. It at once diminished and yet humanized Frank in her eyes. She felt his silent urging for her to obey, and his presence gave her the courage to do as Gordon commanded. Squeezing a dollop of the cold clear gel onto her fingers, she smeared it against her asshole, which was clenched tight.

"Now watch and learn, Frankie boy. I'm going to fuck a girl the only place she deserves to be fucked." Gordon unzipped his pants and stepped neatly out of them. Gina was looking down at the floor and didn't see the sizable erection as he slipped off his underwear. Gordon was considerably aroused from abusing his slave boy. He lusted for the power trip he experienced by dominating both Frank and Gina at once. And on a more secret, less acknowledged level, even to himself, he was angry at Frank, and hurt. He correctly perceived that Frank's feelings for Gina went beyond that of pleasure over use of a toy. In a word, he was feeling like the lover scorned.

Gina cried out slightly as he crouched behind her, gripping her hips. She felt his hard penis head press against her tightly shut sphincter. She knew she had to relax or he would hurt her all the more. She tried desperately to control her fear. She didn't dare try to catch Frank's eye, but she felt his presence in the room and felt safer because of it. Focusing on the relaxation techniques he had taught her, her body eased somewhat. Gordon's thick cock head slipped past the first ring of muscle. Gina held very still, afraid that any movement might hurt her more.

"Slut," Gordon said through clenched teeth, but there was arousal in his tone. He was in his element, with two slaves completely at his mercy. He pulled the trembling woman toward him and his cock pressed further into her ass. It hurt, but wasn't unbearable. Gina found if she could keep her mind empty and let her body flow with Gordon's rough movements, she could tolerate this invasion.

He fucked her hard and fast, leaning over her from behind so that Gina could smell his alcohol-soaked breath. "You like it, don't you, cunt? You know it's what you deserve. I don't like to waste my cum on some twat, no indeed. If I close my eyes, I can almost imagine you're— a—boy!" The last three words punctuated by particularly brutal thrusts which forced a grunt of pain from Gina's lips. She was breathing hard, her breath coming in rasping gasps.

He gripped her long hair, pulling back hard, forcing Gina's head up and back. Her lips were parted and eyes squeezed closed. Frank, from his position on the bed, could see the two of them from the side. He could see Gina's face, her expression at once one of pain, and perhaps something else? The parted lips, the flush—was she experiencing something sexual?

Frank couldn't help but become aroused as he watched his master plunder the virgin asshole of his own personal slave girl. He knew every inch of her, which was now becoming lithe and defined from their daily exercise routine. His hand dropped to his cock, semi-erect and filling now with blood as he watched Gordon thrust hard into the girl, his moan low and sensual.

Gordon collapsed on Gina and she folded under him. He slipped out of her ass, leaving a sticky trail of semen. Gina lay panting and very still, resisting the urge to reach back and touch her very sore bottom. She was like an animal, trapped and remaining still to avoid capture. Of course that was absurd, as she was very much a prisoner with no chance of escape. Gordon groaned and pulled himself to his feet. "Take her back to her room, boy. I forgive you both; consider your slates wiped clean."

Frank, still naked, took his charge by the arm, understanding he was being offered a second chance. This was the first time Gordon had punished him in anger. And by allowing Gina to see him, Frank, naked and impaled by a rubber cock, he had diminished Frank's dominance over Gina. Frank realized with some surprise that this mattered to him. He liked . . . no, that was too weak a word . . . he adored having Gina respond to his every whim, obeying him completely. He had, of course, dominated the other "toys," but mostly he had done so to accommodate his master's wishes. Somehow, this time it was different. He cared what Gina thought. And he cared less what Gordon thought. His motives, he realized, were certainly suspect. Their *object*, their *toy* had become real to him.

He had never voiced his feelings, certainly not to Gordon, and not even to himself on any conscious level. In the past, Gordon had never minded what he did with the toys, as long as he was available, and clearly committed to Gordon. But now his master, aware even before he himself was, was forgiving him for a transgression he hadn't known he was committing. A strange notion had slipped into his brain; did he want to be forgiven?

Chapter 6
THE SPOON

"That's it! You can do it, just five more." Frank's encouragement was punctuated by swats to Gina's bare ass as she completed her step aerobics in front of the ubiquitous mirrors. Gina was bathed in sweat, her body a rosy pink from exertion. The plump exterior had literally melted away with Frank's strict exercise and diet regime, and Gina's body was starting to be defined by shapely muscles and long slender lines.

Today was different from their usual exercise routine, because this time Gordon was in attendance. He rarely bothered to check on Gina's more mundane progress with diet and exercise. His interests lay in her development as a slave and slut. But today, feeling mildly curious, he had decided to watch. He said he wanted to see how Frank was transforming the formerly chubby little girl into the voluptuous woman Gina was becoming. Because Gordon was there, Frank had made the workout especially grueling, and he decided to add a little fun at the end for his master's amusement.

Gina's ass was still ample, and Frank loved to smack the jiggling flesh as she bounced up and down on the stair step in time to the fast tempo music playing on the portable tape deck. Gina wanted to stop; she was nearing the edge of exhaustion, but Frank wasn't done with her yet. "Okay, now for a little weight training. Let's show Gordon how disciplined you are." Gina wiped her brow and pushed her heavy hair from her shoulders. She was trying to catch her breath, and trying to prepare mentally for whatever he had in mind.

Frank looked over at Gordon, who was leaning against a wall, smiling slightly, enjoying the spectacle. Encouraged by the smile, Frank handed Gina a set of arm weights and instructed her to hold them out to either side. After a series of slow lifts, Frank said, "Now let's test your endurance, and your control. I want you to hold these weights out, and stand with your legs spread. I'm going to play with your pussy, and if you fail to hold out the weights at any time, you'll be punished. If you can keep your arms out until I decide the game's over, you win, and you get to come. Easy, right?"

Gina didn't respond and no response was expected. She knew she was being set up to fail and she also knew she had no choice in the matter. Dutifully she held out her weights, with arms already fatigued, and tried to stay still as Frank's sure fingers found her clit and began to massage and tickle her. He inserted a finger, then two, into her pussy. Gina tried to ignore the presence of the laconic Gordon leaning casually against a wall, watching intently, eyes hooded.

Frank's fingers knew their target well, and soon Gina began to breathe heavily. The flush on her cheeks and chest deepened with her arousal, but still she managed to hold out the weights. "Eat her and see how she does," Gordon ordered in a bored voice, though the erection pressing against his jeans gave him away.

Frank knelt, using his hands to spread her shaved pussy for easier access. As the long wet tongue found its mark, Gina started to lower the weights, but somehow found the strength to hold them out a little longer. Frank spread her pussy with his hands, making the stimulation too much to bear. Gina shuddered, and with a sigh of pleasure and defeat, let her exhausted arms fall to her sides. Knowing she'd failed, she let the heavy weights clatter to the floor. Frank kissed and teased her pussy for several minutes until she was on the verge of orgasm, and then he pulled away. "Too bad, sugar. You lose. Now for your punishment."

Coming to herself, humiliated and embarrassed in front of Gordon, but longing for release, Gina pressed her legs together, trying to control her wanton display of need. The two men stared at her, making her blush furiously.

"Very nice, Frank," Gordon said approvingly. "You are becoming quite the sadist yourself, aren't you? I have an idea of how you should punish her." Frank nodded toward him deferentially. Gordon crooked a finger, indicating that Frank should come closer, and he whispered something in Frank's ear. Frank nodded again, raising his eyebrows, but saying nothing. Gina felt a clutch of terror as she tried to blot out various torture scenes that leaped to her mind. Gordon always punished her more severely than Frank, always.

The two men led Gina to her bathroom and Frank said, "How about a nice bath today? You look like you need to lie down a while." Gina was confused; she had expected a whipping or something worse. This must be a time out of some sort before the worst to come. She nodded, grateful for this small reprieve.

When Frank turned on the water, Gina noticed that he didn't add any hot water. The tub was filling with ice cold water. Gina was left kneeling on the floor under the amused gaze of Gordon while Frank left the room. She silently prayed that he would return. He did come back a few minutes later armed with a large bag of ice, which he added to the water. "This should cool you off after that workout, wouldn't you say, Gina? Now get in. This," he paused for emphasis, "is your punishment."

Gingerly Gina stepped into the tub, gasping as her foot touched the cold water. She looked at Frank with an appeal in her eyes, but she didn't protest. She had learned it was useless. She stood for a moment and then lowered herself slowly into the frigid tub, shivering as the water covered her, leaving only her breasts exposed. The nipples quickly puckered, erect with the cold, and Gina began to tremble uncontrollably after just a few moments. The two men watched her tremble as the cold water continued to fill the tub. Her skin flushed pink as her body tried vainly to warm itself. "P-p-please, I can't do this. I beg you." She implored the captors to let her out of the tub.

"I like when she begs, don't you? Slaves should beg, and we, as her masters, decide if we will relent, or let her suffer." Gordon watched her a few more moments, enjoying the look of suffering and pleading on her face. "Let's fuck her, Frank. Let's see what it's like to fuck a frigid bitch." His laugh was cruel. As he spoke, Gordon began to strip off his clothing. His cock was hard. Frank also stripped, and then held out a towel for the freezing, trembling Gina, who took it gratefully. She was barely dry when Gordon pointed to the floor and said, "Kneel, cunt. On your hands and knees."

Frank lay down flat next to Gina, his cock already bobbing eagerly in the air. "Climb on his cock, bitch. I'm gonna fuck your ass while Frank fucks your nasty twat. Move!" Gina scrambled over Frank, who held her icy body by the hips as he guided his cock into her pussy.

"Man, it's excellent! Ice cold body, red hot pussy. Nice." Frank slid his shaft into Gina, moving her so that her juices would flow. Despite her predicament, her icy skin, and her knowledge that Gordon was about to fuck her in the ass, Gina couldn't control the tremor of plea-sure that went through her as Frank eased himself fully into her.

Then she felt Gordon's rough hand on her, pushing her forward so that he could access her ass more easily. Crouching on Frank's legs, Gordon smeared KY jelly on Gina's asshole and then pressed his cock into her. Gina cried out; it felt like she was being split in two, with a large cock in her pussy and an even larger one pressing into her little asshole. Though Gordon had used her anally a number of times now, she still wasn't used to it and she definitely didn't like it!

But Gordon did. He moaned loudly as he began to fuck her, slowly, and then with more intensity. The pressure began to build inside of her from two cocks impaling her at once. The pain of the anal rape was offset by the pleasure of Frank's cock moving inside of her. As so often happened to her with her captors, pleasure and pain were mixed, twirled together in a delicious agony.

Gordon's movements forced her down hard onto Frank's cock. He responded by arching his hips up into her, which forced her back against Gordon. Together they writhed, and Gina's cold body became heated as the two men grunted and sweated over and under her. Gordon came first, clutching Gina by the throat as he did, choking her. Frank came soon after, shooting his hot seed deep into Gina. She was not per-mitted to come, which was a relief to the now truly exhausted woman. The men left her in the bathroom, locking the door behind her. As Frank followed his master out the door, he whispered to her, "You've earned some hot water. Use it. I'll be back later to take you to your room." And he was gone.

• • •

Gordon was away on business and wouldn't be back until tomorrow. Frank knew it was foolish; he knew he was breaking the rules, but he wanted to fuck Gina in a real bed instead of on that hard mattress that she slept on. What would it matter? Gordon would never know; Gina would never tell, Frank was sure.

And so that afternoon, he led his naked girl, her wrists bound in silky rope in front of her, to the master's bedroom. The last time she had been there, she had been brutally sodomized. Her heart was pounding with fear, but when Frank opened the door, there was no blond man with a cruel mouth waiting to abuse her. Frank grinned and said, "The cat's away. Let's play!" Gently he pushed the still confused Gina onto the satin quilt. It was a deep turquoise blue, and the pale lovely Gina looked small and vulnerable against the fabric. She sighed, leaning into the heavenly softness. She had forgotten there could be such luxury, at least for her. But fear of reprisal made her wary. She dared to voice her fear. "Gordon? He isn't here? You're sure? I shouldn't be here. I'm not allowed—"

"You're allowed where I say you're allowed," Frank cut her off. He was a little nervous himself, since the repercussions of what he was doing, should he be caught, would be severe. But somehow he didn't care. He wanted his lover—yes, his lover—here with him in this bed. He untied her wrists and secured a length of silk rope to each wrist separately. Slowly he raised her arms high over her head and secured each wrist to a brass bedpost. He left her legs free.

Frank lay down next to his bound girl and, taking her face in his hands, kissed her deeply. "Do you trust me?" His face was close to hers. Gina nodded slowly. Of course she trusted him. What choice did she have? And what did it matter? Frank must have been thinking along the same lines, because he turned away from her and said, "No. Don't answer that. It was a stupid question. You have no choice. Trust me or not, you're stuck." Frank felt the bitterness of this, like bile in his throat. He knew his feelings were ridiculous. What did he care if she trusted him? She was their prisoner. And it was probably time they started to think about getting rid of her. There was too much emotion involved. It was impeding his relationship with Gordon. It was making him act like an idiot.

He was on the brink of deciding to take Gina back to her room and forget this nonsense when she kissed his shoulder. Something about the gesture, so sweet, and not forced, moved him. He turned toward her, hunger in his eyes, and took her in his arms. He kissed her mouth, her chin, down her neck to her breasts. Gently he bit each nipple. Gina moaned and closed her eyes.

Maneuvering himself so that he was now on top of her, Frank used a knee to spread her thighs, which fell open easily. His cock positioned itself between her legs and he lay heavily across her, enjoying the feel of her soft body. He ran his hands lightly up her arms, still stretched and bound over her head. Using one hand, he adjusted his cock, directing it into Gina's already wet pussy.

Gina sighed and Frank let her hot sweetness engulf him. He focused on her lovely breasts for a while, teasing and suckling her. Then his hands moved up, finding her neck. He lifted his head and whispered again, "Do you trust me?" Again Gina nodded, and this time he decided she must prove it. Slowly his hands closed around her neck, tightening just enough to slightly restrict her air intake.

"Don't resist me. Prove you trust me." Gina closed her eyes as Frank's grip tightened around her throat. Her breathing was shallow now, and she coughed a little as he choked her, but she didn't struggle. He started to fuck her, slowly at first, with his fingers still gripped tightly around her throat.

As his pace and thrust increased, he tightened his hold, and Gina could barely breathe now. She was still, and her eyes were open, watching him, but still she did not resist. He realized he could kill her, easily, with just a slightly tighter grip. The thought perversely aroused him further and he fucked her passionately, calling, "Gina, Gina," with his hands still tight on her throat.

He came hard, and Gina's body arched up into his as he did so, but her eyes were closed, mouth slack. Had he gone too far? His heart was pounding crazily from the intensity of his orgasm. He let go, and could see the imprint of his fingers, red against her throat. But she was breathing, and her little breasts swelled prettily with each breath. He was overcome, looking at his tethered darling, who hadn't struggled, who had trusted him

Gently he kissed her mouth. Then he carefully released her bonds and enfolded her into his chest. Without being aware of it, they drifted off to sleep in the master's bed. How could they have known his trip was cut short, and that he was driving home at that moment, eager to see his slave and his toy?

"What the fuck is going on here!" Gordon burst through the door and the startled lovers jerked apart, Frank leaping to his feet, penis dangling and half erect, Gina curling into a ball at the head of the bed, hiding her face on her knees. "In my bed! Here you are like, like . . ." he stopped, refusing to say the word *lovers*, but the word hung unspoken in the air like a ripe apple dangling from a tree.

Gordon sat heavily on a chair and fumbled in his pocket, producing a package of cigarettes and a lighter. He lit one with hands that seemed to tremble slightly, and then took a deep drag on the cigarette. Frank looked down, and mumbled, "Excuse me, Sir. I meant no harm—"

"Shut up! I don't want to hear your bullshit excuses!" Frank looked down, biting his lips to keep from speaking. He knew that the cigarette was a bad sign, as Gordon had been trying to quit. Gordon turned his angry gaze from Frank to Gina, who huddled, terrified. "Go get Gina's spoon, Frank." He didn't look at the taller man as he spoke. Frank hastily left the room and retrieved the spoon that had been used for oral training. He handed it to Gordon, knowing what was ahead, wishing he dared to protest.

"Lie down, slut. On your back, hands over your head. Do as you're told or it'll be that much worse." Gina did as Gordon ordered, trying to keep her body from trembling. "Hold her down, boy," Gordon commanded. Frank knelt on the bed near Gina's head, placing his large strong hands on her arms to hold her still. Gordon sat down next to the naked woman and took another drag on his cigarette, so that the ash glowed red. Stubbing out the butt, he removed his lighter from his shirt pocket and flicked the flame to life.

Gina watched without understanding as he heated the silver bowl of the spoon. The flame blackened the underside of it where it touched the metal. "Hold her," he said, and without further preamble, Gordon touched the heated metal to the white underside of Gina's bare breast. He held it there as Gina screamed. He kept it there until her screams converted into sobs. As Gina thrashed wildly, Gordon calmly held the flame again against the spoon, enjoying the look on Gina's face as she watched him reheat the spoon for the other breast.

Again he burned her flesh, and now sobs became screams again, her anguished cry shrill and echoing in the room. Frank's face spoke of his own suffering, but still he held the poor naked woman who writhed on the mattress. "Now get her out of here, Frank. We need to talk."

Frank carried the hysterical woman to her room. This wasn't the first time Gordon had used the spoon, but it was the first time Frank had felt the burn as if it had been his own flesh. Poor innocent Gina, punished because of what Frank had done. Something would have to change. He realized it finally, or admitted it finally. Something would have to change. He couldn't do this anymore.

Their talk consisted of Gordon wondering aloud what was happening to his slave boy. He informed Frank that they would be getting rid of Gina soon, and making a move, maybe in a couple of weeks. Frank didn't protest. What could he say? Frank had expected a terrible punishment of his own, but none was forthcoming. Instead, Gordon seemed to withdraw.

He stayed longer hours at work, and would call sometimes at the last minute to inform Frank, who was waiting with dinner prepared, that he wouldn't be home until much later, and not to wait up. He never explained where he was, and Frank didn't ask. He had never questioned what Gordon did when he was away; he was the slave after all; how could he question his master?

Gina, however, was not so lucky. Gordon began to use her more often, devising more bizarre and dangerous games. His favorite pastime was to fuck her ass, using her roughly until she bled. One day he entered her room and said, "Gina, are you afraid of needles?"

"Sir?"

"I said, are you afraid of needles? A simple question. Answer it."

"Yes, sir." She already dreaded whatever was coming, though she hadn't yet imagined what it might be. She was to find out.

"Good. I like it when you're afraid. I'm going to pierce your nipples today. And no, Frank won't be here to hold your hand."

"Oh, please, sir, I'm begging you—"

"Good. I like it when you beg. You're going to be begging a lot, I imagine, before this day is over. Now, I don't want you wiggling around while I do this, so I'm going to tie you down." He pulled over the doctor's exam table they sometimes used to tie down their toys. "Get up. Do it, cunt, or I'll whip you first and then pierce you. All the same to me. Do what you're told. Now!"

Reluctantly Gina climbed up on the table, laying down, feeling almost numb with fear. Gordon secured her wrist cuffs and ankle cuffs, now worn and soft from constant use. He snapped the clips in place and quickly attached her to the table, rendering her completely immobile.

"You want this, don't you, cunt? Say yes."

"Yes, sir," she lied, and he knew it, but it didn't matter.

"You want me to take this sharp, long needle and pierce your tender nipple, don't you, cunt? Say yes, and say it like you mean it."

"Yes, sir."

"Yes, what?"

She gulped, forcing herself to say the words he demanded, hoping it would elicit some shred of compassion from the sadistic madman who held her captive. "Please, sir, I want you to pierce me. Please, sir, please." The please lingered in the air, and they both knew she was begging for something else, something she wasn't going to get.

Gordon took a long hollow needle from a wooden jewelry box he had brought in. "This really doesn't hurt that much. Not that much. It'll be over in a flash, and then I'll give you a pretty gold loop to keep it open while it heals. Won't that be lovely, Gina? Much nicer than those barbell things some masters seem to favor. This is real gold, too. Only the best for my cunt." He held it up for her to see, a lovely little gold hoop that glittered in the light.

Gina was breathing shallowly and fast now; she couldn't seem to catch her breath. Gordon's cock swelled nicely in his pants as he watched the terror in her face and the needle drew close to her breast. Taking a nipple and pulling it taut, Gordon pushed the sharp point against flesh, forcing it through as Gina screamed, a long anguished wail. Her body thrashed involuntarily, but she was too immobilized to move, and he completed the work calmly, sliding the gold loop through her newly pierced nipple, allowing it to snap into place.

When he took hold of the other nipple, Gina's eyes rolled up and she fell back in a dead faint. Unperturbed, Gordon pierced the other nipple and slid in the second nipple ring. He stood back admiring his work. Leaning forward, he slapped the still bound woman in the face until she roused, moaning. Her nipples ached and burned. She looked down to see the gold rings nestled in nipples red and engorged from the trauma.

"It's done, slut. Your titties look much better now. I should have done this ages ago. Now the real fun begins." He released her bonds and told her to get up and move to the center of the room. When she was standing, legs trembling, under the pulley apparatus, he said, "Don't move." He took two long gold chains from the box and secured each one to the loops at her breasts. Carefully, he extended the loops and secured them to the pulley, causing her nipples to be pulled taut by the chains. Gina cried out as her freshly pierced nipples were pulled upward. She stood on tiptoe, trying desperately to relieve the tugging pressure, but Gordon just laughed and tightened each chain a fraction more, making her cry out again.

"Don't worry. As long as you're still, they won't rip. But if you struggle—" He left the warning unsaid, but it was clear that she risked tearing her own flesh if she resisted the chains that bound her. "Now, you've been trained well enough to stay still for what is coming. Nothing too bad, really. I'm just going to cane your ass a bit, while you count for me. I'm sure you can stay still for that, can't you, cunt?"

"Please, sir," Tears spilled as she watched him take the dreaded bamboo cane from its case. He brought it round to her face, and she tried to kiss it, but instead began to cry and beg.

"Now stop or I'll have to gag you, and I don't want to do that. I want to hear you scream. Only ten, and you can surely handle that, can't you, Gina?" He didn't give her time to answer, but went around behind her, swishing the cane through the air.

It whistled and landed with a *thwack* against her ass. Gina jerked forward, straining her tender nipples against their chains. She screamed.

"Count," he ordered.

"One," she managed to say between clenched teeth.

Swish and, "Two." Gordon was precise, hitting her neatly from the top of her ass down to her thighs, creating a crisscross of welts as he went. Gina was crying loudly now, but somehow she managed to stay still. If she jerked, she might indeed rip her nipples, and the thought terrified her into taking the blows, barely moving.

"Ten!" she screamed, and, thank God, he stopped. She waiting, panting and sobbing, for him to release her, but he didn't. He simply left the room, leaving her hanging by her nipples, on tiptoe, ass on fire.

That's how Frank found her about an hour later. He dropped the plate of food he was holding, and gasped, "Oh my God." Gordon hadn't told him what he had done to her. Frank stared, taking it in—the naked woman tethered by newly pierced nipples, her head hanging, eyes closed as if she were dead. Running to her, he took her head in his hands and whispered, "Gina? Gina! Are you all right! Shit! What did he do?"

Slowly she opened her eyes, staring at Frank as if she didn't know who he was. Quickly and carefully he released the chains from the pulley and helped Gina to her mattress. She rolled to her side, moaning, and he saw the cruel welts that covered her ass, which was crisscrossed with long red marks. Frank got some salve and carefully massaged it into her flesh. Then he had her lie back while he examined her breasts. "Well, I have to admit, he did an excellent job. He's done it before a number of times. But always with willing slaves who wanted it done. I know he didn't give you a choice, did he? Of course not," he said as she slowly shook her head.

Frank sat down near Gina, holding a glass while she sipped with a straw, gratefully drinking the cool water he offered. He stared into her pretty face, pale with exhaustion from her ordeal. He had to confide in someone, and there was no one else.

"Listen, Gina." He paused a moment, gathering his thoughts, making up his mind. "Things are getting too weird here. It's never been like this before. I mean, we've had our differences, but no one's ever gotten between us before. They were toys. Plain and simple. We'd use them a while and then get rid of them. Set them free. Sometimes they wanted to stay, but we'd make them go. We've been together for years now, Gina. And it always worked.

"But not anymore. Something's gone wrong with Gordon. I don't know how else to describe it. He barely talks to me now. And if I'm completely honest, something's different with me, too. It isn't a game anymore. Maybe that's what it is. It isn't a game. You aren't a toy." He looked at her, but Gina had turned her head away. He was sure she was listening though. He was sure she was listening hard.

"I know that sounds crazy. Of course none of them were toys. But to us that's what they were. Playthings to be used and discarded. But Gina, you—" He stopped, afraid to say what was in his heart. Instead, he said, "Nothing has ever come between us before, me and Gordon. But now it's as if he doesn't want me anymore. And I, well, I don't know that I want him. There! I've said it." Frank looked around, almost as if he expected Gordon to come charging into the room, to challenge him to a duel or something equally ridiculous. But Gordon didn't come.

Frank took one of Gina's limp hands in his. "I've never felt afraid for a toy before, but I'm afraid for you. Gordon's been hurt, and he's going to hurt back. That's always been his M.O. I think he knows the best way to hurt me is by hurting you." Gina looked at him now, and he flushed, turning away.

"What I'm trying to say, Gina, is I think I need to get you out of here. Gordon's planning a change soon; it's just a matter of time. I've tried to talk about us, his and my relationship and what's happening, but he won't talk about that either. He just gets angry and leaves. I don't know what to do. You know Gordon can be a little crazy some-times." He smiled ruefully. Who knew better than Gina how crazy Gordon could be? What Gordon might do next was a real danger, and they both knew it.

"Get me out?" she dared to ask. Frank smiled, relieved to hear her speak. Her face wasn't quite so pale now, and she breathing normally. He touched one of the gold loops that pierced Gina's nipple and she flinched slightly but didn't pull away.

"Yes. I'm going to help you escape before he dumps you some-where, bound and gagged and naked. I'm not going to let that happen this time. But then I'm going, too. The game is over. I've got savings. Gordon's been supporting me for years, and I have extensive invest-ments in my name only. I'm going to make a fresh start. I'm going to leave the country. Now, I'm trusting you with this. Gordon doesn't actu-ally own me, of course, but I think he will try to stop me, if he suspects. It isn't even that he wants me to stay anymore, but his pride won't allow him to just let me go.

"I have to get you out first. God knows what he'd do to you if I left you here." Gina shivered and clutched herself. Frank took her gently in his arms. "I'm going to set you free, Gina. You can go home."

• • •

Gina sat up in her room, humming softly, tunelessly, thinking about what Frank had told her. She hadn't been able to sleep, or concentrate on anything since he left. He was going to set her free! She would see her mom and dad! She would see Dwayne. She tried to think about Dwayne, to imagine his face. She realized with a bit of a shock of horror that she couldn't remember his face. Not in detail. She knew what he looked like, but she couldn't imagine the face.

How could she go home to them now? How could she possibly tell them what she had been through? How would they understand what had happened inside of her? Not only was her body changed—the obvious changes from dumpy to slender, with nipples pierced and bejeweled, and the less obvious changes of sexual maturity and the loss of her virginity—but also her mind and heart. She knew Dwayne would reject her out of hand for having lost her virginity, even if it was rape. He might pretend otherwise, but she knew him too well.

But even if he took her back with open arms, even if he *forgave* her for the sin of being kidnapped and sexually tortured, it was her mind that had been changed even more than her body. She would never be the same innocent girl who questioned nothing and accepted whatever her father decreed for her as *God's will*. She questioned everything now. Where she used to accept everything at face value, now she was deeply introspective. She had basically lived a life of contemplation and meditation, albeit enforced, for the past several months she had been held captive.

While her mind had stilled, deepened, her body had been awakened. She could admit now, without shame, that she loved being fucked, she loved taking a cock deep into her throat, she loved the feel of a wet mouth against her pussy. She even—dare she admit it—needed the whippings now. They were part and parcel of her sexual experience. They defined and heightened the pure pleasure of what Gordon disdainfully referred to as vanilla sex. She could no more separate the experiences of pleasure and pain than she could separate her mind and body. It was all one to her now.

Could she possibly share any of this with Dwayne? With her parents? Would they have the slightest glimmer of understanding? Of course they wouldn't, nor could she blame them. This bizarre experience was totally outside of their ken. And yet, if she didn't return to them, where would she go? What would she do? She had no money; she had no friends to speak of. She had nothing. Nothing but Frank, who said he was leaving her, leaving the country.

She realized with a heart wrenching and sudden certainty that she didn't want to leave Frank! How could that be? She was being given the chance to escape, and she didn't want to go, not without him. But he hadn't made that offer. He didn't want her. He wanted to wipe his slate clean and start afresh somewhere far away. Far from Gordon, and far from her, the one who caused the rift between slave and master.

Chapter 7

THE BEGINNING

Frank bided his time until Gordon's upcoming business trip at the end of the week. It would last three days, and that would give Frank time to do what had to be done. While doing the grocery shopping earlier in the week, Frank had been to his bank, where he had closed his account and withdrawn several thousand dollars.

At home, he began to pack the things Gordon wouldn't notice were missing, like his own financial statements and records, and some of his off-season clothing. They both kept a packed bag ready at all times, since one never knew when they would have to escape. They were, after all, criminals, kidnappers, always living on the edge. The place and everything in it were rented. They went from location to location, and Gordon always had work, since he was a consultant to investors who liked how he tripled and quadrupled their money with his skill and attention to the market. He didn't need a set location to do that in; just his laptop and his brains.

The day Gordon said goodbye, barely glancing at Frank, he wasted no time. All he planned to take was his clothing and a few books and CDs. He would start new wherever he ended up. His first ticket would be to Winnipeg, Canada, where he had family. He would decide from there what to do.

But Frank's heart was heavy. While he felt no misgivings at leaving Gordon, who had been his partner, if you could call him that, for the last seven years, he felt deeply saddened at the thought that he wouldn't see his Gina anymore. No, not his. She had never been his, never been there out of her own free will. It was just a game they played. You could never truly own another, certainly not by force. They could only belong to you if that gift was offered freely. He and Gordon had been thieves for years. Stealing other people, treating them like objects and then dumping them. But Gina was real, and Frank was going to give her the best gift he could by letting her go; setting her free.

Surely she would run and never look back. She would probably call the police in, or certainly her parents would. Who could blame them? He knew Gordon would leave as soon as he realized what had happened. He probably already had another location in mind; he was always a step ahead, which was one reason they had never been caught.

When Gina awoke that morning, she saw something by the door. Clothing! It wasn't the clothing she had when they kidnapped her. The old shapeless dress and practical shoes were long gone. Instead, there was a pair of soft denim jeans and a pink sweatshirt. There was also a large leather bomber jacket, lined with fleece. And next to these items was a pair of silky underwear that was nothing like the waist high cotton briefs she used to wear, a pair of socks, and some white sneakers.

Gina fingered the garments for a few moments, wondering if she dared to put them on. This must be the moment! Frank was going to release her. She felt her heart start to thump with excitement. It was really going to happen! Quickly she pulled on the panties, the pants, which fit perfectly, and the oversized sweatshirt. The fabric tickled her sensitive nipples, still bearing their gold hoops. It felt so strange to be wearing clothes after all this time! She would have to get used to it again. She put on the socks and pulled on the new sneakers, just her size. The shoes were perhaps the hardest thing to get used to; they felt like blocks of cement on her feet. She held the jacket in her lap and sat down to wait.

Nothing happened. An hour passed. Two hours passed, and no Frank! What was happening? Had Gordon come home unexpectedly? Would he burst in at any second and beat her within an inch of her life for wearing clothes? When was Frank coming! What would she do?

She stood and paced, her brow furrowed with worry, her hands clenched with nervous energy. If only he'd come open the door! The door. She approached it slowly, as if it might reach out and grab her. Slowly, slowly, she extended her hand, and touched the shiny knob. It turned. She pulled and the door opened. She forgot to breathe as she looked out into the hallway that had defined her universe these past months.

She listened for a sound, some evidence that there were other people in the house. Silence. "Frank," she called, but it came out as a whisper. She stepped out a little into the hall, alone for the first time outside of her room since her captivity had begun.

"Frank," she dared, a little louder. No answer. She didn't call for Gordon. If he was there without Frank, her life was as good as over anyway. Carefully she tiptoed out of the room and ventured toward the living room. No one. Slowly she walked toward their bedroom. The door was ajar. The bed was made and everything looked in order as far as she could see.

"Hello?" she called, still terrified of being discovered out of her cage and fully dressed. Several minutes later she had combed the small house and there didn't seem to be a soul there except for her.

"Oh God, what do I do?" She remembered Gordon's warning that they were in the middle of nowhere. Where was Frank? He had said he was going to take her away, set her free, not leave her here! She looked out the kitchen window on an impulse and that's when she saw the taxi.

Its engine was running and there was a driver inside. Turning the knob of the kitchen door, hands shaking, she ventured out into the cold winter air, pulling her jacket close around her.

The driver saw her and opened his door, startling her. "Hello, miss," he said, smiling pleasantly. "The gentleman said you'd be out by and by. I didn't mind waiting, seein' how he's paid me so well. Where do you want to go, ma'am?"

Gina stared at him. The old gentleman didn't look like a madman, but rather like someone's grandfather. This was the *getaway*. This was how Frank was setting her free. He had deserted her. Numbly she climbed into the car. The driver climbed back into his seat and eased the cab out of the driveway. It was surreal. She was free!

"Where to, young lady?"

Somehow Gina found her voice. She was dazed and could barely think. She said, "Do you know where Hampton Hills is?"

"Oh sure. Nice area. You want to go there?" Numbly she nodded and stared out the window. She slipped her cold hands into the deep pockets of the lovely jacket Frank had left for her. There was something there. An envelope. She pulled it out and opened it with trembling fingers.

Inside she found a one-way plane ticket to Winnipeg, Canada. There was a phone number in thick magic marker on the envelope, and several hundred dollars, in twenties, tucked between the onion thin pages of the ticket itself.

"Excuse me, sir? I've changed my mind. Take me to the airport."

Finis

My Secret Life
Anonymous

Over two million copies sold!

Perhaps the most infamous of all underground Victorian erotica, *My Secret Life* is the sexual memoir of a well-to-do gentleman, who began at an early age to keep a diary of his erotic behavior. He continues this record for over forty years, creating in the process a unique social and psychological document. Its complete and detailed description of the hidden side of British and European life in the nineteenth century furnishes materials for the understanding of the Victorian Age that cannot be duplicated in any other source.

The Altar of Venus
Anonymous

Our author, a gentleman of wealth and privilege, is introduced to desire's delights at a tender age, and then and there commits himself to a life-long sensual expedition. As he enters manhood, he progresses from schoolgirls' charms to older women's enticements, especially those of acquaintances' mothers and wives. Later, he moves beyond common London brothels to sophisticated entertainments available only in Paris. Truly, he has become a lord among libertines.

Caning Able
Stan Kent

Caning Able is a modern-day version of the melodramatic tales of Victorian erotica. Full of dastardly villains, regimented discipline, corporal punishment and forbidden sexual liaisons, the novel features the brilliant and beautiful Jasmine, a seemingly helpless heroine who reigns triumphant despite dire peril. By mixing libidinous prose with a changing business world, *Caning Able* gives treasured plots a welcome twist: women who are definitely not the weaker sex.

The Blue Moon Erotic Reader IV

A testimonial to the publication of quality erotica, *The Blue Moon Erotic Reader IV* presents more than twenty romantic and exciting excerpts from selections spanning a variety of periods and themes. This is a historical compilation that combines generous extracts from the finest forbidden books with the most extravagant samplings that the modern erotica imagination has created. The result is a collection that is provocative, entertaining, and perhaps even enlightening. It encompasses memorable scenes of youthful initiations into the mysteries of sex, notorious confessions, and scandalous adventures of the powerful, wealthy, and notable. From the classic erotica of *Wanton Women*, and *The Intimate Memoirs of an Edwardian Dandy* to modern tales like Michael Hemmingson's *The Rooms*, good taste, passion, and an exalted desire are abound, making for a union of sex and sensibility that is available only once in a Blue Moon.

With selections by Don Winslow, Ray Gordon, M. S. Valentine, P. N. Dedeaux, Rupert Mountjoy, Eve Howard, Lisabet Sarai, Michael Hemmingson, and many others.

The Best of the Erotic Reader

"The Erotic Reader series offers an unequaled selection of the hottest scenes drawn from the finest erotic writing." — *Elle*

This historical compilation contains generous extracts from the world's finest forbidden books including excerpts from *Memories of a Young Don Juan*, *My Secret Life*, *Autobiography of a Flea*, *The Romance of Lust*, *The Three Chums*, and many others. They are gathered together here to entertain, and perhaps even enlighten. From secret texts to the scandalous adventures of famous people, from youthful initiations into the mysteries of sex to the most notorious of all confessions, *Best of the Erotic Reader* is a stirring complement to the senses. Containing the most evocative pieces covering several eras of erotic fiction, *Best of the Erotic Reader* collects the most scintillating tales from the seven volumes of *The Erotic Reader*. This comprehensive volume is sure to include delights for any taste and guaranteed to titillate, amuse, and arouse the interests of even the most veteran erotica reader.

Confessions D'Amour
Anne-Marie Villefranche

Confessions D'Amour is the culmination of Villefranche's comically indecent stories about her friends in 1920s' Paris.

Anne-Marie Villefranche invites you to enter an intoxicating world where men and women arrange their love affairs with skill and style. This is a world where illicit encounters are as smooth as a silk stocking, and where sexual secrets are kept in confidence only until a betrayal can be turned to advantage. Here we follow the adventures of Gabrielle de Michoux, the beautiful young widow who contrives to be maintained in luxury by a succession of well-to-do men, Marcel Chalon, ready for any adventure so long as he can go home to Mama afterwards, Armand Budin, who plunges into a passionate love affair with his cousin's estranged wife, Madelein Beauvais, and Yvonne Hiver who is married with two children while still embracing other, younger lovers.

"An erotic tribute to the Paris of yesteryear that will delight modern readers."—*The Observer*

A Maid For All Seasons I, II – Devlin O'Neill

Two Delighful Tales of Romance and Discipline

Lisa is used to her father's old-fashioned discipline, but is it fair that her new employer acts the same way? Mr. Swayne is very handsome, very British and very particular about his new maid's work habits. But isn't nineteen a bit old to be corrected that way? Still, it's quite a different sensation for Lisa when Mr. Swayne shows his displeasure with her behavior. But Mr. Swayne isn't the only man who likes to turn Lisa over his knee. When she goes to college she finds a new mentor, whose expectations of her are even higher than Mr. Swayne's, and who employs very old-fashioned methods to correct Lisa's bad behavior. Whether in a woodshed in Georgia, or a private club in Chicago, there is always someone there willing and eager to take Lisa in hand and show her the error of her ways.

Color of Pain, Shade of Pleasure
Edited by Cecilia Tan

In these twenty-one tales from two out-of-print classics, *Fetish Fantastic* and *S/M Futures*, some of today's most unflinching erotic fantasists turn their futuristic visions to the extreme underground, transforming the modern fetishes of S/M, bondage, and eroticized power exchange into the templates for new sexual worlds. From the near future of S/M in cyberspace, to a future police state where the real power lies in manipulating authority, these tales are from the edge of both sexual and science fiction.

The Governess
M. S. Valentine

Lovely Miss Hunnicut eagerly embarks upon a career as a governess, hoping to escape the memories of her broken engagement. Little does she know that Crawleigh Manor is far from the respectable household it appears to be. Mr. Crawleigh, in particular, devotes himself to Miss Hunnicut's thorough defiling. Soon the young governess proves herself worthy of the perverse master of the house—though there may be even more depraved powers at work in gloomy Crawleigh Manor . . .

Claire's Uptown Girls
Don Winslow

In this revised and expanded edition, Don Winslow introduces us to Claire's girls, the most exclusive and glamorous escorts in the world. Solicited by upper-class Park Avenue businessmen, Claire's girls have the style, glamour and beauty to charm any man. Graced with super-model beauty, a meticulously crafted look, and a willingness to fulfill any man's most intimate dream, these girls are sure to fulfill any man's most lavish and extravagant fantasy.

The Intimate Memoirs of an Edwardian Dandy I, II, III
Anonymous

This is the sexual coming-of-age of a young Englishman from his youthful days on the countryside to his educational days at Oxford and finally as a sexually adventurous young man in the wild streets of London. Having the free time and money that comes with a privileged upbringing, coupled with a free spirit, our hero indulges every one of his, and our, sexual fantasies. From exotic orgies with country maidens to fanciful escapades with the London elite, the young rake experiences it all. A lusty tale of sexual adventure, *The Intimate Memoirs of an Edwardian Dandy* is a celebration of free spirit and experimentation.

"A treat for the connoisseur of erotic literature."
—*The Guardian*

Jennifer and Nikki
D. M. Perkins

From Manhattan's Fifth Avenue, to the lush island of Tobago, to a mysterious ashram in upstate New York, Jennifer travels with reclusive fashion model Nikki and her seductive half-brother Alain in search of the sexual secrets held by the famous Russian mystic Pere Mitya. To achieve intimacy with this extraordinary family, and get the story she has promised to Jack August, dynamic publisher of *New Man Magazine,* Jennifer must ignore universal taboos and strip away inhibitions she never knew she had.

Confessions of a Left Bank Dominatrix
Gala Fur

Gala Fur introduces the world of French S&M with two collections of stories in one delectable volume. In *Souvenirs of a Left Bank Dominatrix*, stories address topics as varied as: how to recruit a male maidservant, how to turn your partner into a marionette, and how to use a cell phone to humiliate a submissive in a crowded train station. In *Sessions,* Gala offers more description of the life of a dominatrix, detailing the marathon of "Lesbians, bisexuals, submissivies, masochists, paying customers [and] passing playmates" that seek her out for her unique sexual services.

"An intoxicating sexual romp." —*Evergreen Review*

Don Winslow's Victorian Erotica
Don Winslow

The English manor house has long been a place apart; a place of elegant living where, in splendid isolation the gentry could freely indulge their passions for the outdoor sports of riding and hunting. Of course, there were those whose passions ran towards "indoor sports"—lascivious activities enthusiastically, if discreetly, pursued by lusty men and sensual women behind large and imposing stone walls of baronial splendor, where they were safely hidden from prying eyes. These are tales of such licentious decadence from behind the walls of those stately houses of a bygone era.

The Garden of Love
Michael Hemmingson

Three Erotic Thrillers from the Master of the Genre

In The *Comfort of Women*, the oddly passive Nicky Bayless undergoes a sexual re-education at the hands (and not only the hands) of a parade of desperate women who both lead and follow him through an underworld of erotic extremity. The narrator of *The Dress* is troubled by a simple object that may have supernatural properties. "My wife changed when she wore The Dress; she was the Ashley who came to being a few months ago. She was the wife I preferred, and I worried about that. I understood that The Dress was, indeed, an entity all its own, with its own agenda, and it was possessing my wife." In *Drama*, playwright Jonathan falls into an affair with actress Karen after the collapse of his relationship with director Kristine. But Karen's free-fall into debauchery threatens to destroy them both.

The ABZ of Pain and Pleasure
Edited by A. M. LeDeluge

A true alphabet of the unusual, *The ABZ of Pain and Pleasure* offers the reader an understanding of the language of the lash. Beginning with Aida and culminating with Zanetti, this book offers the amateur and adept a broad acquaintance with the heroes and heroines of this unique form of sexual entertainment. The Marquis de Sade is represented here, as are Jean de Berg (author of *The Image*), Pauline Réage (author of *The Story of* O and *Return to the Château*), P. N. Dedeaux (author of *The Tutor* and *The Prefect*), and twenty-two others.

My Secret Life	$15.95	The Uninhibited	$7.95
The Altar of Venus	$7.95	Disciplining Jane	$7.95
Caning Able	$7.95	66 Chapters About 33 Women	$7.95
The Blue Moon Erotic Reader IV	$15.95	The Man of Her Dream	$7.95
The Best of the Erotic Reader	$15.95	S-M: The Last Taboo	$14.95
Confessions D'Amour	$14.95	Cybersex	$14.95
A Maid for All Seasons I, II	$15.95	Depravicus	$7.95
Color of Pain, Shade of Pleasure	$14.95	Sacred Exchange	$14.95
The Governess	$7.95	The Rooms	$7.95
Claire's Uptown Girls	$7.95	The Memoirs of Josephine	$7.95
The Intimate Memoirs of an		The Pearl	$14.95
Edwardian Dandy I, II, III	$15.95	Mistress of Instruction	$7.95
Jennifer and Nikki	$7.95	Neptune and Surf	$7.95
Burn	$7.95	House of Dreams: Aurochs & Angels	$7.95
Don Winslow's Victorian Erotica	$14.95	Dark Star	$7.95
The Garden of Love	$14.95	The Intimate Memoir of Dame Jenny Everleigh:
The ABZ of Pain and Pleasure	$7.95	Erotic Adventures	$7.95
"Frank" and I	$7.95	Shadow Lane VI	$7.95
Hot Sheets	$7.95	Shadow Lane VII	$7.95
Tea and Spices	$7.95	Shadow Lane VIII	$7.95
Naughty Message	$7.95	Best of Shadow Lane	$14.95
The Sleeping Palace	$7.95	The Captive I, II	$14.95
Venus in Paris	$7.95	The Captive III, IV, V	$15.95
The Lawyer	$7.95	The Captive's Journey	$7.95
Tropic of Lust	$7.95	Road Babe	$7.95
Folies D'Amour	$7.95	The Story of O	$7.95
The Best of Ironwood	$14.95	The New Story of O	$7.95

ORDER FORM
Attach a separate sheet for additional titles.

Title	Quantity	Price

Shipping and Handling (see charges below) _____

Sales tax (in CA and NY) _____

Total _____

Name _____

Address _____

City _____ State _____ Zip _____

Daytime telephone number _____

❏ Check   ❏ Money Order   (US dollars only. No COD orders accepted.)

Credit Card # _____ Exp. Date _____

❏ MC   ❏ VISA   ❏ AMEX

Signature _____

(if paying with a credit card you must sign this form.)

Shipping and Handling charges:*

Domestic: $4 for 1st book, $.75 each additional book. International: $5 for 1st book, $1 each additional book
*rates in effect at time of publication. Subject to Change.

Mail order to Publishers Group West, Attention: Order Dept., 1700 Fourth St., Berkeley, CA 94710, or fax to (510) 528-3444.

PLEASE ALLOW 4-6 WEEKS FOR DELIVERY. ALL ORDERS SHIP VIA 4TH CLASS MAIL.

Look for Blue Moon Books at your favorite local bookseller or from your favorite online bookseller.